Other People

Moya Roddy

WORDSONTHESTREET

First published in 2010 by

Wordsonthestreet

Six San Antonio Park,

Salthill,

Galway, Ireland.

web: www.wordsonthestreet.com

email: publisher@wordsonthestreet.com

The moral right of the author has been asserted.

A catalogue record for this book is available from the British Library.

ISBN   978-1-907017-05-6

Cover design, layout and typesetting: Wordsonthestreet
Cover image: *Silhouette* © Antonyesse – Dreamstime.com
Printed and bound in the UK

Other People

ABOUT THE AUTHOR

Dubliner Moya Roddy left school at 17 and attended the National College of Art and Trinity Arts Lab as a night student. She continued painting during a two-year stay in Italy, before moving to London where she trained as a television director at the Soho Poly. *Que Sera Sera,* which she wrote and directed, won a Sony Award in 1983 and the British Film Institute commissioned a full-length feature, *I Prefer Freesias* in 1985. Several of her screenplays were optioned in America. She worked in television adapting a novel for Scottish TV and in Current Affairs/Documentaries for Channel 4 on programmes such as *Promised the Earth,* analysing the UN Decade for Women and was sole writer on the innovative four-part art series *Opening Up the Family Album.*

Returning to live in Ireland, her debut novel *The Long Way Home, (*Attic Press 1992), was described as 'Simply Brilliant' in the Irish Times. They had published her first short story, *Biddy's Research,* in 1991 and since then she's had numerous stories published including *The Day I Gave Neil Jordan A Lift* (*Anthology of Irish Comic Writing,* Penguin/Michael Joseph,) which was broadcast by RTE and CBS Canada. Her work has been anthologised in *Dublines* and the *Anthology of Irish Women's Writing*, (Bloodaxe). She wrote several episodes for RTE's sit-com *Upwardly Mobile.* A radio play *Dance Ballerina Dance* was short-listed for the PJ O'Connor Award and broadcast by RTE. She collaborated with Pete Mullineaux on *Butterfly Wings,* broadcast on RTE radio in 2010, and two stage plays, *Trust Games*, (Galway Youth Theatre 2002) and *Red Lorry Yellow Lorry–* specially commissioned for the 2003 Cúirt International Festival of Literature. She completed an MA in Writing at NUIG in 2008.

Moya combines her writing with facilitating meditation at Brigit's Gardens, Roscahill, GMIT and the National University of Ireland. She also teaches a workshop *Writing With Heart* uniting writing skills with meditation techniques.

To Pete and Cassie

Acknowledgements

The author would like to acknowledge the following journals and anthologies in which some of the stories included here first appeared:

So Very English (Serpent's Tail); *Virgins and Hyacinths* (Attic Press); *!Divas! (*Arlen House); *Quiddity International Literary Journal; Ropes; WOW! Anthology* (Wordsonthestreet).

Contents

Alice

The room was a sun-trap. Sprawled across her bed, Alice wallowed in the muggy heat. Too hot, almost. Eyes half-closed, she watched the black speck on the curtains take flight, collide with a pane of glass. Trapped too, unless she opened the window. Buzzzz, buzzzz ... Hard to believe something so small could make such a racket. In some countries people ate them. If she ended up locked in this room, with no food, would she stalk the insect? Squash it with a finger and gobble it down? No, they'd die together, the fly squat on her cheek, her final companion. Sometimes it was nice imagining herself dead. Dying anyway.

'What are you doing lying there with your uniform on?' Her mother materialised in front of her.

'Thinking,' Alice answered.

'Well think outside. All that lovely weather going to waste.'

'But -'

'No buts. And open a window.'

If her mother died would she eat her? Unbuttoning her school uniform, Alice shuddered away the thought.

'Jelly on the plate, jelly on the plate ...
Wibbly wobbly, wibbly wobbly
Jelly on the plate.'

Alice peered. It seemed miles and miles to where Regina and the rest of her gang were skipping. Why couldn't she stay home? There was no law

9

saying you had to go out. And the dress she'd changed into made her feel as if she might blow away. It let the sun and wind at her. The elements. Different from what was inside a kettle. "Cover the element," her mother would shout. Otherwise the kettle might burn. Blow up. Would it explode in a ball of flames? Burn the house down? For a moment the kettle blazed, tendrils of fire sprouting like the trailing roots of her mother's spider plant.

'Alice, Alice!' Regina called.

Alice pretended not to hear; turned her head in the opposite direction, wishing the ground would open up and swallow her. But she was too big. Bigger than the houses, bigger than the road, her head touched the sky. She felt her face burn. Like the inside of a kettle when there wasn't enough water.

'Alice, c'mere!'

Inching down the road, Alice had the strangest sensation of growing smaller and smaller.

'Hold the rope, you can have a turn later.'

Alice did what she was told, letting on she didn't see the smirk on Yvonne's face that said she wouldn't get a go later, that when it came to her turn, they'd stop, invent another game. All the same, she held the rope, allowed the swishing sound, the singsong chant, the blurred words of the skipping rhymes soothe her. It was nice playing, even for a little while.

"I had a little dolly,
I left it on the shelf,
Would you believe, would you believe
It walked away itself..."

The rope caught Regina's leg.

'You did that!' the girl flamed.

'Did what?' Alice faltered.

'Held the rope too tight.'

Spiteful smiles split her playmates' reddened cheeks, glittered in their puffed-out eyes.

'You - made - me - out -,' Regina prodded the younger girl's chest.

Alice bit her lip.

'Cry-baby!' her tormentor exulted, dancing with glee. 'Cry-baby, cry-baby,' the others yelled, howling and spitting in delight.

'I am not,' Alice hissed, tears wetting her face.

'Who wants to play with you anyway?' Regina's mouth curved. 'C'mon, let's go to my house.' Nose in the air, she led the way, the others following in mock procession.

Alice watched them as they flounced up the road. Then she blinked and they disappeared.

Alice ventured into the half-finished housing estate, eyes on sticks for grown-ups. The builders, "cowboys" her daddy called them, had disappeared one day, never come back. She'd been warned about going there but if she went home early her mother would blame her for not knowing how to play, for being too sensitive. Sensitive. She'd seen the word on a tube of sun-cream. For skin that burned easily. Would she burn easily? Her eyes burnt, smarted with unshed tears. Dodging in through a gap, she found herself in a maze of rooms, each one identical with grassy floors carpeted in fuzzy-headed dandelions. "Clean up that mess," a voice in her head shrilled. Picking up a stick, Alice scattered the weeds, gazing in awe as seed-heads rose in a cloud, like snow falling upwards. 'One o'clock, two o'clock,' she chanted, windmilling through the fairy clocks. Eerily, they swarmed round her, attaching themselves to her clothes, her hair, drifting into her mouth. Swatting them away, Alice fled down a long, narrow corridor. Reaching the back door, she skidded to a halt, her feet teetering at the edge of an enormous crater. Then with a cry, she plunged headlong into the brown, clammy earth.

Alice stared round her. The hole she'd landed in had a tunnel at one end with an enormous slab of granite standing guard at the entrance. Marching up to it, Alice clicked her heels, saluted. Thousands of tiny, glassy eyes glinted at her from the surface of the rock. 'May I?' she joked, ducking past. The tunnel wasn't high and Alice had to bend double as she made her way through the dark shell. A clayey smell filled her nostrils. When she'd ventured as far as she dared, she hunkered down, wrapping her arms round herself for warmth, her head resting on her knees. Goosebumps dimpled her bare arms. A tear trickled. Opening her mouth, she caught it with her tongue, tasted salt. Why did the other girls pick on her, it was not as if she did anything. A noise like seagulls squawking filtered into the dim interior. Maybe it was children's voices. Regina's mother might have shooed them out. Alice closed her eyes. If they found her, Regina would claim the tunnel, do "one potato, two", make sure she won. She won everything, did everything her way. When they played tag, Regina was never 'it'. And when they cooked potatoes, she grabbed the good ones, left the burnt ones for everyone else. Fingers in her ears, Alice rocked. She'd die rather than let them find the tunnel.

Alice fumbled for the bedside lamp, shrieking as her fingers touched something slimy, crumbly. Her head bumped against the ceiling. Where was she ...? Where? In the tunnel, that's where. She must have fallen asleep. Why was it so dark? Alice opened and closed her eyes several times but the darkness stayed. She couldn't see anything, not even her own body. How would she find her way out? Alice swallowed. She was going to have to feel her way, use her hands. Groping along the squelchy, oozy earth, she tried not to think about crawling things, worms and beetles, things she didn't even know the name of. At last, her fingers latched onto something solid. The stone, she'd reached the stone! Cool air brushed her cheeks. Glancing up, she saw the sky was full of stars. Her parents would kill her. Where did they think she was? Why weren't they out looking for her? A scurrying noise made her cry out. She clutched a hand to her mouth, afraid of drawing whatever it was towards her. A mouse, she prayed, a mouse, not a rat. A murderer, a voice in her head taunted. Not a murderer, she was too young to die. Terrified, Alice curled into a ball, gritting her teeth as pins and needles attacked her legs. A scream cut the night. Alice heard it. She tried to stop the sound but it was too late. Now she'd started she couldn't stop. On and on she screamed. She didn't care if someone killed her. She wanted someone to come, anyone, she didn't want to be alone a second longer.

Light.

Light coming in her direction. Voices.

'Aliiice! Aliiice!!! Can you hear us? Alice? Answer!'

Torches flashed like giant cats' eyes.

'Mammeee, Daddeee,' she yelled running towards them.

'Oh thank God, thank God!' her mother answered, dazzling Alice's eyes with her torch.

'It's her, it's her, it's Alice!' people chorused. A cheer went up. Another. She recognised some of the adults: Regina's father, Yvonne's older brother – people from the bottom of the road. Her mother's arms loomed, pressed her close. She could feel tears, hot against her cold cheeks.

Her father reached for her, hoisted her up on his shoulders. 'My little girl,' he crooned, his voice so soft Alice thought it might break.

For a few days, Alice was a heroine: kids at school pointing, whispering. But it was wearing off. At lunchtime everyone in the playground had laughed when Regina shouted: "Go back to the dirty hole you crawled out of". They hadn't laughed the other night, Alice thought, slipping through the makeshift gates into the building site. She knew she'd promised not to but the urge to go back was too strong. She needed to go. Making her way round the back of the houses, her heart swelled at the memory of the cheers. She felt warm all over like she was sitting in front of a huge fire, could feel its hot breath on her skin.

'Look what the cat dragged in.'

Seeing Regina, Alice's mind somersaulted.

'You're not allowed here your mammy said, so go home,' the girl gloated, her face red from dragging a sheet of corrugated iron.

'What are you doing with the corry?' Alice demanded.

Yvonne's head popped out of the tunnel.

'What does it look like? We're making a den. We've got cushions and a carpet.'

'The tunnel's mine, I found it.'

'Excuse me! Did anyone see Alice's name on the door?' Regina scoffed. 'Better go and see your solicitor.'

Alice went hot, cold, stared at the ground. When she glanced up the other girl had a fishy grin on her face.

'You can come in if you bring something.'

'What?' Alice asked, smelling a rat.

'We're going to cook some food but we haven't any matches. You could go to your house and get some.'

Alice nodded. She'd have to be careful though, if her mammy found out there'd be murder.

Regina struck a match. The wick in the primus flared, went out. She struck another. This time it held a few moments.

'It's probably wet,' Trish sighed.

'Too windy, there's a draught coming in.'

'We could use the corry as a door,' Yvonne suggested.

'We won't be able to see, eigit.'

'Course we will, with the stove.'

'Alice, put the corry against the door.'

'Why me?'

'Last in, that's why. You know the rules.'

'Smell's gone,' Yvonne shouted.

Outside, Alice picked up the corrugated iron, heaved it across the entrance.

'I can't get in,' she called.

'Penny's dropped,' Regina jeered. 'Who wants you anyway?'

Hearing the girl's words, something hard planted itself in Alice's chest. It took up residence, pushing against her ribs. Everyone wanted her the other night. Everyone. As she leaned against the tall stone that stood guard, the hardness grew and she wondered if it was possible for people to turn into stone. Sounds of squabbling, laughter came from the tunnel. They'd forgotten her already. 'It's not fair!' she whispered, 'not fair.' She stayed on, wanting to give them time to change their minds. As she waited, her fingers traced the glittering sequins on the surface of the stone and the glassy eyes winked back: we're your friends, they seemed to say, we can help you.

Alice pressed her back against a wall of earth. If she could dislodge the stone it might topple. Using her feet, she pushed and pushed. The stone swayed. Taking a deep breath, she gave a last shove, cheering inwardly as the boulder tipped over, half-blocking the entrance, enough so they couldn't get out. Serve them right! Now they were trapped. Now they'd have to beg her for a change. As she waited for the high-pitched voices to stop and someone to notice, Alice felt a twinge of unease. What possessed her do such a thing? There was no way she could move it back on her own. She'd have to get help. And if Regina told, there'd be trouble. A whiff of burning singed the air. Alice licked her lips, felt her mouth dry as she backed away. Best scram; say she went straight home. Voices were calling now, yelling, hands rattling the corry. Sweat broke out on Alice's forehead as she raced through the empty house. They'd probably just burned potatoes like last time, that was all. She could still hear them yelling at the gates. The screams reminded her of cheers. The cheers for her. The further away she got the louder they seemed: screams and cheers fusing until she couldn't tell which was which. And she could see them. The bright faces of her mother and father, all her neighbours. Cheering her. They loved her. Loved her. She wouldn't go back. Wouldn't even look back. They could scream all they wanted to. Let them scream.

'Aliiiiiccce, Aliiiiiicce, Alliiiiicce!'

Let them scream.

Let them.

Other People

Yes! Yes! Yee-ess!! Second prize, second bloody prize! Fuck the begrudgers! He'd done it! Why the hell hadn't he opened the shaggin' thing as soon as it arrived! Terrified of losing, that was why. Reaching into a cupboard, Bernard pulled out a whiskey bottle, emptied the dregs into a glass. 'To me,' he toasted, his eyes soaking up the words on the flimsy sheet of paper, savouring every nuance: highest quality ... difficult decision ... eight hundred entries ... With each phrase Bernard's heart swelled. Award ceremony ... meal ... presentation of prizes ... a well-known, **internationally** known playwright to do the honours. He threw the letter into the air. Maybe it was a cliché to say people were over the moon but that's just how he felt. Over the sun and bloody stars as well.

Adopting a swagger, Bernard crossed to what he called his den, a box-room with a computer and filing cabinet stuck in one corner. The previous day, he'd printed out the first draft of a new three-acter. Selecting the top page, he began to read aloud, trying to give the correct weight to each sentence, pause. The lines tripped off his tongue whereas yesterday they'd seemed thin, unconvincing. He made a face. Could his news really make that much difference? Eight hundred was some validation. Of course, writers were their own worst enemies. Take the play that had just got second. He'd been on the verge of chucking it at one stage. The ending alone had cost him months of agonising.

Especially after Maeve had advised changing it. Good job he'd stuck to his guns. The wrong ending might have fucked it. From now on he'd trust his own instincts.

The sea was calm as Bernard strode along the Prom, an earlier decision to ring Maeve on hold. He wanted time to relish his success, enjoy privately what it felt like to be a winner, extract every ounce before it became common property. Leaning on the parapet, his thoughts turned to Miller's *Death of a Salesman;* to the moment when Willy Loman discovers that Bernard, the boy he'd assumed had no future, is going to try a case at the Supreme Court: "The Supreme Court and he didn't even mention it!" The shock and pain in those lines never failed to touch a raw nerve at Bernard's core but it was the reply that rubbed the salt in: "He don't have to - he's gonna do it." What he wouldn't give to be that other Bernard, the one who didn't have to parade his dreams because they'd already come true. The fact they shared the same name had always struck him as a good omen although in most productions the emphasis was on the second syllable - Ber*nard* - making it sound different, exotic. Well, he might not be going to the Supreme Court, but he was going to a dinner, a prize-giving - influential people would be there. For once he'd be on the inside track. All round him the sea swelled, the suck and rush sounding like applause. Bernard took a metaphorical bow. In the water, his reflection rose and fell, then, as the waves dispersed he watched his shadow image break up, scatter. Without regret, he waved it goodbye, conjuring up a new self, one he'd always suspected lurked beneath the surface, waiting for others to recognise.

'Second place? Brilliant! Wow!' Raymond Walsh sniffled, shook his head vigorously to clear it.

Keeping it to himself had proved harder than Bernard had anticipated. He'd managed a whole hour, the news burning a hole in his chest.

'Second,' Ray repeated, 'who won, anyone we know?'

Trust Ray to get the boot in. Couldn't let him have his fifteen seconds of fame. Bernard steered the conversation in a more agreeable direction.

'Looks like Shepard or Mamet might be giving the prizes, some big-shot anyway.' It was a small lie and the letter had said 'internationally known'.

'Probably on holidays at the same time.' Ray cleared his throat. 'Gotta run, great news, don't forget I knew you before you were famous.'

Fuck you too, Bernard thought. Some people weren't big enough. He'd have to get a move on; now Ray knew it would be all over the city in an hour. Less. In ten minutes people would be telling him about it! With a spin. *Second prize*, he could still hear the nasal inflection. Checking his watch, Bernard realised it was lunchtime. He'd better go to Sweeney's, see if Maeve was there. She'd never forgive him if she heard about it from someone else. Crossing the bridge, he quickened his pace, suddenly anxious to see her, needing to share his news with someone who'd understand what it meant.

Alone in a window seat, Maeve's face had an intense faraway expression. During their ill-fated attempt at living together, Bernard had discovered this usually meant she was organising something mentally, working out arrangements.

'Skiving off?' she asked as he eased in beside her. He slipped the letter into her hand. Halfway down the page, she threw her arms round him. 'I'm so pleased!' There was soup on her breath. Carrot and coriander: one of their favourites.

'You deserve it. How are ye feeling?'

'Took me two hours to open the bloody thing. Couldn't hack another rejection.'

'Oh, Bernard, you're such a good writer, it really pisses me off.' She leaned into his ear. 'Know your problem, you care too much about other people.' She squeezed his arm again. 'What'll it be? My treat. Pint, soup, both?'

'Pint, don't think I could eat.'

He bunched up to let her out. As soon as she'd gone he noticed a small feeling of deflation. Her words were meant to be encouraging but they'd stung all the same. In truth he didn't believe he was that good; he needed other people to convince him.

'The champagne will have to wait 'til I'm paid,' she quipped, arriving back with his drink.

'I should have bought you one.'

'Chalk it up for when you get the money. Course, once you start hob-nobbing with the rich and famous you'll forget all about us.'

Bernard took a long slug: forgetting was the last thing on his mind. All he wanted to do was sit tight, bask in everyone's admiration. The liquid washed down his throat. He felt cavernous; there was enough room inside him to sink a bloody ocean. 'Believe in yourself, that's the main thing,' Maeve whispered, clinking glasses. 'Would you look who's walked in! Kieran! C'mere. Go on Bernard, tell him.'

Bernard held onto the bar while the pub swirled round his head. Any minute, he thought, the whole place could take off in a puff of smoke. His eyes searched the nearest faces. Who the hell was this shower of bollix? 'Slainte,' he said, raising his glass to a couple of passing girls.

'Did ye win the Lotto?' one of them asked. The taller of the two made a face, giggled. 'D'ye know who you're talking to - the greatest-' Bernard stopped, distracted by the tiny bubbles in his pint. He held the glass at arm's length, watched the bubbles, trapped in froth, pop and vanish. Pop, pop! One day, he'd vanish too and no one would notice. He had to find Maeve. There were things he had to tell her. Pushing through the crowd Bernard felt seasick at the sight of so many mouths opening and closing. What the fuck did they have to say to each other?

'Congrats!' A hand slapped him on the back.

'Yeah, yeah, thanks.'

Finding an empty snug, he sank down on the worn velvet upholstery. His eyes drooped. Outside, the babble grew louder and he began to feel sorry for himself, sorry for the stranger he'd turned into. He needed Maeve. She knew him. When he opened his eyes, she was standing in the archway, blurry, like a badly taken photograph.

'Scuttered! Sure, why not? Want a short?'

'Sit beside me. Maeve?'

She hesitated.

'Please.'

Bernard concentrated, trying to remember what it was he wanted to tell her.

He held up his glass. 'D'ye see? The bubbles, trapped. Gone, pop!'

'All right Wittgenstein. C'mon. Time to get ye home.'

'The bubbles, see?'

'Yes, the bubbles.'

He put his pint down. 'Did I ever tell you about my father? About the day I saw him?'

'What day?'

'What day?' he mimicked, looking at her shrewdly. 'You're not patronising me are you?'

'No, Bernard, I'm not.'

'I hate people fuckin' patronising me. Just like my father, bastards patronised ... D'ye know the play?'

'What play?'

'*The* play, Miller ... What was I saying? The father, Loman, Willy Loman?'

'Death of a Salesman?'

He looked at her, shut his eyes briefly, opened them. 'You always know what I'm talking about, don't you?'

Maeve smiled.

'Ber*nard!*' he emphasised the second syllable. 'Ber*nard!* Am I shouting?'

She shrugged. 'What's this got to do with your father?'

Bernard's glazed eyes studied her. What the hell was she talking about?

Bernard groaned, squashing his temples between his hands in an effort to ease the pain. He groaned again as isolated moments from the previous night began to surface. How in Christ had he got home? And Maeve. What had they been talking about? God, he hoped he hadn't asked her to sleep with him. Sloughing off the duvet, he heaved himself onto the floor. As his feet hit terra firma, the ghost of his dead father gained substance. He might have guessed. Whenever anything good happened, he could always count on Holmes Senior to put in an appearance. Never let me forget, will ye Dad? Holding his head, he padded to the bathroom. What age had he been – nine, ten? One of those birthdays anyway. Mad into cowboy pictures. His mother had taken him to a Western earlier. Bernard pointed two fingers at the image in the bathroom mirror: 'Bang, bang. You're dead.' Blowing away an imaginary puff of smoke, he made his way to the kitchen, filled a pint glass with water. Tossing it back, he crossed to a window, just as he must have done all those years ago, impatient for his father to come home, dying to tell him about the film, to worm out the present secreted in an inside pocket. 'Come away from there,' his mammy called, but Bernard ignored her, staying put, intent on dashing out as soon as he saw his daddy. Crouching beneath the sill, his eyes combed the street, deserted except for one of the Roche girls pushing a pram. Then the garage door opposite shot up and Mr Duggan and a man he'd never seen before edged out, lugging a sheet of metal. Doing a nixer, Bernard thought. He wasn't sure what nixers were but his mammy said they paid for holidays. The other thing she said was that Bernard's daddy was too honest for his own good and should get off his high horse. Bernard didn't like her saying that but his daddy told him the important thing was not to mind what other people said. "A right cowboy," he called their neighbour and Bernard could tell that men like Duggan were beneath his father's contempt. The boy scrutinised the mechanic. With a fag hanging from his mouth and oily smudges on his cheeks he could easily be a baddy in a film. He watched the men hoist their load onto a lorry, then the stranger took out a pack of cigarettes, gave one to Duggan and the two of them lounged against the gate, smoking. Bernard cocked an imaginary pistol. Swivelling to take aim, he spotted his father at the top of the road – no mistaking the jaunty steps, the cap askew. If this were Tombstone, his daddy would challenge those outlaws to a gunfight. The boy fixed on the approaching figure but as Mr Holmes drew level, his footsteps became less jaunty and a weird expression crept into his face. Bernard raised a hand to shield his eyes but he couldn't stop looking, couldn't stop seeing his daddy, *his daddy,* shove a hand in his pocket, shuffle, then smile at Duggan and the stranger, *smile* and tip his cap as if those gangsters were running the show. Backing away, Bernard saw how the men barely acknowledged his father, carrying on as if he wasn't there. Fighting tears, he sped downstairs. If he could, he'd have killed those men stone dead. Instead, he charged out the back door, headed for the woods. It was late when he came home, his mother's eyes were red and his daddy roared at him but he didn't care. Racing upstairs, he ignored the brightly-wrapped present on the kitchen table.

Lost and forgotten whatever it was, Bernard thought, moving from the window. How much had he understood as a boy, how much had been embellished over the years? There was no way of knowing. One thing was certain: his father and him had grown apart and when Bernard had set his heart on becoming a writer, Mr Holmes had made it clear he disapproved. Acceptance - was that what Bernard longed for? But from whom?

The prize-giving was over in a flash. The applause, his own beaming face, the speech he'd rehearsed for hours so much history as he hesitated in the entrance to a plush-looking lounge awash with light. Animated faces, caught in the gleam of chandeliers, talked and drank and laughed; the atmosphere was charged, glitzy, everything he'd imagined. He'd actually shaken Ayckbourn's hand, joked with him. Well, almost.

'You spoke very nicely.' Ringed fingers pressed his arm, 'That line you quoted - so apt.'

'Thanks. *Death of a Salesman*.' Bernard avoided eye contact. The last thing he wanted was to get stuck with the middle-aged woman who'd received a special mention. Excusing himself, he made for the bar, changing his order to spirits when he realised it was free. Over the rim of a double whiskey, he scanned the crowd trying to figure out who was who. The expression 'work the room' popped into his head but he'd no idea how to go about it, where to start. Afraid of looking conspicuous he attached himself to a loosely-knit group, eavesdropping on their conversation, although they were talking so loudly it was hardly necessary.

'Shame Mamet couldn't come. Apparently he was asked. Ayckbourne's a bit-'

' - I know. Still, he is the most popular playwright since Shakespeare. English anyway.'

'Have you heard the Americans have invaded, talent-spotting according to the grapevine.' The woman speaking nodded towards a huddle of men in sober suits. Bernard followed her gaze. Finishing his drink in one gulp, he ordered another. What would other people do, he wondered?

'Glad you could make it. I'm Richard, remember?' The man's smile went on and off like a light bulb, not quite making it to his eyes. 'Come in, take a seat. Sam will be down presently.'

Bernard shuffled past. At this hour of the morning the American accent grated.

'Can I get you something? Coffee, water?' He gave the impression of standing on tiptoes.

'Coffee would be great. Thanks.'

Richard disappeared into an adjacent room. Bernard inspected his surroundings. He'd been expecting something more opulent but it had the same decor as his own: a kind of international bland.

'Nice ceremony, great people,' Richard enthused, handing him a chunky hotel cup.

Bernard touched his forehead: 'One too many,' he joked.

Richard gave him a puzzled look, lapsed into silence. Bernard stirred the coffee, instant, from the watery look.

'Sam liked your play.'

'He's read it already?' Bernard hadn't time to hide his surprise.

'Sam doesn't like to waste time. He's been up since five. Don't quote me, but .. he feels it might have movie potential.'

The coffee burnt Bernard's tongue. Shit! He hadn't realised they were film people.

'Sam wants to shoot the breeze a little, get the lie of the land.' He jumped to his feet as an older, rugged-faced man entered the room.

'Bernard isn't it?' Sam emphasised the second syllable.

Irrationally pleased, Bernard grinned.

'Get home okay last night? Course you hadn't far to go.' Sam looked at his assistant who laughed obligingly. Bernard joined in, a little too loudly.

The young man produced a second cup of coffee. Sam drained it, before stretching out on a sofa, hands clasped behind his head.

'Good script. I liked it. You got talent. Take it from me.'

The space between Bernard's ears expanded, filled with buzzing.

'Course the ending stinks.'

The buzzing stopped. The ending? He loved the ending. He'd

worked his guts out on the ending.

'It'll have to go. Straight down the toilet. But hey, I'm jumping the gun, let's hear your thoughts.' The film men exchanged sidelong glances. 'Writing for the screen's a little different to what you do,' Sam continued, 'it's more a collaborative kind of thing. Some writers can be very possessive.'

'Well, I'm glad you liked it ...,' Bernard played for time, his gaze straying out the window to the throngs of pedestrians navigating the thoroughfare; the stalled cars. 'The ending ... personally, I feel ... Don't get me wrong. I'm not saying it's perfect. It's not perfect. It needs work. But, if you take the central idea, I mean - what other ending's possible...?'

Sam stuck a toothpick between his teeth. The seconds ticked. Removing it, he snapped it in two before turning to Bernard. There was a smile on his face, a kind of knowing smile, sad.

'I've been at this game all my life, son. You're a playwright. I respect playwrights. From where I'm sitting, they do it for love. Let me tell you something. Making films is a tough business. Want a little advice? Might be worth your while allowing other people be the judge of what works.'

'Sam has some pretty cool ideas,' Richard chipped in. 'Like to hear them?'

Bernard didn't answer. In the street, a man in paint-spattered overalls had caught his attention. Striding along, he stood out from other passers-by, his steps big, bouncy, just as his father's had been all those years ago. Unmistakable.

In the hotel room, the two Americans continued to trade ideas but Bernard saw past their amiable expressions, recognised the smug faces of Duggan and the stranger, knew he'd go on seeing those faces the rest of his life, unless ...

Bernard opened his mouth.

'Agreed?' Sam was on his feet. 'Good. For a second, I thought we were gonna lose you.'

'More coffee?' Richard hovered.

'Something stronger. I think this guy's one of us. What do you think Bernard?'

How Quietly The Water Laps

Paradise the brochure had promised: an unspoiled oasis of sand, sea and blue unchanging weather. Fun too. Throughout the year Kerry, Sal and Orla had talked about nothing else, spending their free time shopping for the perfect dress, the matching ear-rings and shoes, the bikinis and swimsuits, suntan lotion and after-tan milk, together with bag loads of extras which might come in handy.

The airport hadn't looked promising as the plane circled, but the moment the trio swanned down the gangway onto melt-hot tarmac, shedding garments the way animals shed skin, they sensed Kalachas would live up to their expectations. The previous year, they'd gone package; this time they were going to find their own apartment. Buoyed by a beginning of holiday feeling, they decided to splurge on a taxi. The driver, tanned, surly, cap skew-ways, drove off at blood-curdling speed, showering a queue of waiting backpackers with dust. The friends caught each other's eyes as the car hurtled recklessly along a corkscrew road, front wheels perilously close to the edge. Let him drive recklessly, their glances agreed, in this foreign country they were protected by the gods. Safe in this unspoken belief, they giggled helplessly, the driver grinning at them through the rear mirror, encouraged by their behaviour to drive even faster.

In the days that followed, the young women tested out their belief,

25

taking on the might of the ocean ravishing the rocky coastline, yelling and screaming in abandonment and pleasure, their pale skins and rainbow swimsuits transforming them into strange exotic fish. Ducking and diving, they pitted arms and legs against the waves crashing about their heads. Afterwards, exhausted and becalmed, they floated, trusting in the beneficence of the water to hold them in its lap before depositing them gently on skin-tingling sand. Infused with sun and sea, their faith acted like a lubricant, seeping into every pore, making them stretch and expand like cats in sunshine.

The apartment they rented was large, self-contained, one of a pair on the roof of a taverna perched at the water's edge. It was more expensive than they'd expected, but memories of the previous years with boorish lads grabbing their towels as they raced, wet and shaking, from lukewarm communal showers, were still vivid. On their first evening, Thanos, their landlord, had pointed out a table in the restaurant, telling them proudly that as residents it was reserved for them. No one else would be permitted to eat there, he'd assured them, unless the signorinas decided to eat elsewhere. At the thought, Thanos had thrown up his hands, rolled his eyes. Later, witnessing a procession of people being turned away, the young women congratulated themselves on their choice, their luck. The gods were definitely on their side.

What drew crowds to the taverna was not the food or even the starched white linen that hung on makeshift lines each morning like ghosts trapped in sunlight. Pierre was the unlikely magnet. Middle-aged, stocky, with a scar running down his left cheek, tourists, particularly women, could not get enough of him. During the day, while other waiters - lanky adolescents with teeth and tans to die for - lounged in brightly-coloured T-shirts and shorts, Pierre sported a crisp white shirt, dickey-bow, pressed black trousers. The younger men sucked up to customers, flirting or placating them, Pierre kept a distance. When he did serve, customers felt special, chosen. 'Pierre,' diners called, 'Over here, Pierre!' At first the friends were at a loss to understand but as Pierre's spell began to work they found themselves trying to catch his eye; pretending they weren't ready to order if another waiter came scurrying over. He had a knack of remembering what they drank; if the place was quiet, he'd arrive, off his own bat, with a pastis for Kerry, oozo for Sal and Orla. Without smiling, he'd set them on the table, withdraw. When they realised he did the same for other holidaymakers, a tiny cloud blotted their horizon. Not everyone, they consoled themselves, just a favoured few like themselves. On these occasions, Orla would try and charm him into conversation, using her hands when words failed. Pierre refused to be drawn, backing away each time, always polite, always with a bow. Little by little, he became a subject of conversation, of speculation, the kind that knits a holiday together, fills the empty spaces. They discussed him at length, lazily, enjoying the sight of other customers, single women especially, vying for his attention. Before long - later - no one could remember how or from whom or whether they'd made it all up - they seemed to know everything about him, although what was rumour and what had a grain of truth remained a mystery. His real name was Christopholos, Pierre was a souvenir of a sojourn in Paris where he'd worked at a famous restaurant. He was from one of the islands, Crete or Corfu were favourites. Crucially, he had a fiancee stowed away, pining, while he saved enough money to set up his own business. The scar: a duel over his or another man's fiancee; revenge for some shady drug dealing which had caused him to flee France. Lacking romance, the possibility of something as mundane as an accident was never considered. Whatever the truth, Pierre worked hard. Other waiters came and went but Pierre was always there: mid-morning when the trio stumbled bleary-eyed to breakfast, in the early hours when they staggered back from a club. One night, from the shadow of the stairwell, they watched him polish glasses in the deserted restaurant, the muscles in his back visible through the thin cotton of his shirt as he bent silently over his task. In bed, they mused on how vulnerable he'd looked, lonely even, how he must resent fate for keeping him from his lover, how unfair life was; filling in the blank reaches of his life with their own unconscious longings.

Day in, day out, with Pierre as a fixed point, the friends traipsed from taverna to beach, beach to taverna, laden with towels, lotions, bottles of water; lulled by an unchanging sun, time measured only in the darkening of their skin.

'How is your fiancee?' Orla asked as Pierre set three glasses on the table. It was late afternoon and they had him all to themselves. Sal, who'd slipped off her shoes, nudged Kerry with a bare toe. All three held their breath. For a moment, it seemed he might dodge away, but instead, after a quick glance round, he unfastened the top of his shirt, pointed to a cross hanging round his neck.

'A present?' Orla shaped a box with her hands.

'To keep me safe,' Pierre explained, fingering it.

The friends exchanged knowing glances.

'From other women?' Kerry ventured and Sal had to turn away to keep a straight face.

He puzzled over the words before slowly shaking his head.

'Is she beautiful?' Orla asked.

'She get old,' he frowned, then as if regretting this sudden intimacy, shoved the cross back inside his shirt and buttoned up.

His gaze rested on the three young women, lingering almost imperceptibly on Orla. With a small smile he indicated the drinks. 'Present,' he said, walking away.

As the doors to the kitchen swung shut, Orla's friends broke into peals of laughter.

'He fancies you, he fancies you!' Sal and Kerry squealed, delighted with the development.

'Shut-up,' Orla hissed, 'he'll hear you.'

'He doesn't understand,' Sal retorted. 'Bit past it though. Must be nearly fifty.'

'Life in the old goat,' Kerry gloated.

Orla glared. 'Grow-up, both of you!'

In mock horror, her friends clapped their hands to their mouths. 'Orla fancies him,' they told each other, bug-eyed.

Despite her tan, Orla blushed. 'I'm going for a walk,' she muttered, banging down her glass.

Reaching the water's edge, Orla paused. Tiny rivulets streamed round her toes. She peered down at the bits of sea-washed wood, tiny shells, wisps of seaweed drifting on the water's lilt: flotsam and jetsam spewed up to rest a moment on the shoreline. How quietly the water laps, she thought. Aeons ago, we clambered out of water, maybe on such a still, gentle evening. Sadness overwhelmed her. She didn't fancy Pierre, she was interested, sympathetic. Dimpling the sand with a toe, she traced a question mark. Of course, she liked the thought of him fancying her, it made her feel important, special. She turned the question mark into a heart. All right, she admitted, there was an attraction but it was really the sun and the sea that were working their magic. Relieved by the admission, she turned and waved to the others.

Conversation over dinner was sporadic, forced: oases of chatter, little bursts of laughter punctuating silence. Orla was self-conscious as Pierre served but he seemed unaffected, treating them in his usual manner. On the other side of the restaurant, Juliet and Lynn, a couple of thirty-something women from England, were celebrating their last night. Way past their sell-by date, Kerry had gibed, the first time the trio had bumped into them.

'She's got darker foundation in her cleavage,' Sal poked Kerry, surreptitiously pointing at Juliet.

'Better watch out or she might take off in a high wind,' Kerry spluttered.

Orla joined in half-heartedly, tired of the banter that hid their own desperation. They were enjoying the holiday but they'd be going home soon and nothing had happened. Exactly what was meant to happen was never discussed, there was no need, woven as it was into the attention they paid their bodies, the posing and promenading, the long hours dancing, sweating, getting pissed; the hopeful glances.

Towards the end of the meal, a commotion broke out at the English women's table. The friends watched, round-eyed, while Juliet tried to persuade Pierre to have his photograph taken with her. When he attempted to pull away she snaked an arm round him, urging Lynn to snap.

'Go on, give her a kiss,' one customer yelled. Other diners laughed.

Near the entrance to the kitchen, the younger waiters made crude gestures. Orla thought she understood. In their own country, women like Juliet wouldn't give Pierre a second glance; flirting with him, with any of them, was just part of the holiday.

Eventually, one of the waiters shouted something in Greek; with a shrug Pierre acquiesced, draping a reluctant arm round the woman, staring blankly at the camera. In the after-effect of the flash, Orla thought she caught a glimpse of another face, charged, angry.

'She's stolen your fella,' Sal whispered then noticing the look on Orla's face changed tack. 'All set for the disco girls? Only forty-eight hours left.'

'Not going!' Sal and Kerry shrieked in unison.

'I think I'll go to bed early, read a book.'

Kerry squinted suspiciously at Orla then went back to repairing her make-up. 'You haven't arranged a little rendezvous?' she teased, sucking in her cheeks to apply more blusher.

'Don't be daft.'

'Shit! Now, I look sunburnt,' she screamed.

Sal offered a tissue. 'Hurry up, we don't want to get there too late.'

'You both look fantastic!' 'Don't wake me if I'm asleep,' Orla added.

The pals stopped by the door, urging their friend one last time to get dressed, come, but it was half-hearted, each sensing a night apart might be best thing. Night sounds wafted up from the street below and Kerry and Sal grinned expectantly: with only two of them, who knew what might happen?

Alone, Orla brooded, returning in her mind to the water's edge. This time it had the opposite effect, unsettling her. Getting out of bed, she crossed to a window, leaned out. The sound of the sea was palpable. Only one thing for it, she decided, pulling off her nightdress.

The beach was deserted, the breeze from the ocean sending a shock of goose-pimples up her arms, a tingle through her body. Breaker after breaker tumbled and crashed on the sand. With a shout she ran in, gasping at the collision of skin and water. After swimming a few yards, she realised the tide was stronger than it looked but before she could do anything, she found herself being dragged then hoisted aloft by invisible wet fingers. Instinct told her to go with it; she had a sensation of being swallowed, then just when she thought she might be sucked even deeper, the wave flipped her over and she found herself back on the beach. She tried again, this time keeping level with the shore but the sea tossed her about, just as she'd once seen a cat toss a helpless shrew for the sheer fun of it. Back on dry land, she shook herself like a dog, 'I give in,' she called, 'you're bigger,' then remembering a game she played as a child she stood in the water to see how long she could remain upright before the swell knocked her flying. An incoming wave flooded over her, flicking her off her feet but she bounced up again. She felt puny but in her element. Again and again, she braved the sea until exhausted, she threw herself on the sand: this was what she'd take home with her, this was what she'd remember.

Back at the apartment, blood pumping through every cell, Orla felt conscious of her body as a living, breathing entity. She felt an urge to move, strut, exhibit this wondrous thing. It wasn't midnight. If she took the shortcut along the beach she could be at the club in fifteen minutes. From the wardrobe, she chose a silky sarong that clung like a second skin. A quick twirl in front of the mirror and she was out the door. Halfway down the fire escape, she stopped. Pierre was sitting in the darkened restaurant, staring out to sea, the red tip of his cigarette glowing. Ask him, a voice prompted. She hesitated, then afraid of losing her nerve, coughed. Startled, Pierre put the cigarette behind his back like a schoolboy.

'Wanna come to the club?' she asked, doing a little dance with her hips in case he didn't understand.

'Too old, too old,' he shook his head.

'No, you're not,' Orla protested. Feeling bolder, she took his hands, tried to draw him from the chair. He resisted, making her tug. As they play-acted, she noticed the sweatshirt and light-coloured trousers he was wearing showed his bulk: without his uniform he looked his age, less attractive. Orla shrugged the thoughts away. What did it matter, she'd still be the envy of everyone at the disco.

'Okay, okay,' he relented, getting to his feet. 'I like Ireland.'

Unsure if he meant her or the country, Orla laughed.

They took the short cut. Conscious of being alone with him for the first time, Orla chattered about the holiday, conveniently forgetting Pierre couldn't understand. Once they reached the beach, she shook off her sandals, walked barefoot on the velvety-soft sand, cool, liquid almost. She noticed Pierre was wearing lace-ups, the kind older men wear. A grain of disappointment lodged in her heart. As the path petered out, they veered inland towards the dunes. Orla stopped to put on her sandals. When she straightened, Pierre was standing behind her – she could feel his breath on her neck. Neither moved. When their lips met, she returned the kiss, hoping to rekindle the feelings she'd had earlier by the water's edge. Pierre lowered her to the ground, murmuring endearments, the words sounding foreign, romantic. She allowed herself drift on the rise and fall of his desire, but it was someone else kissing her hair, her eyes, her breasts. 'No!' she cried out, suddenly alert, 'no!' pushing at Pierre's hand as he tried to force her legs open, the metal of his belt cold where he'd raised her dress. Imprisoned beneath his weight, she wriggled, squirmed, beat at his back. Pierre, absorbed in the thrust of his own body, seemed oblivious. 'Stop! Stop! I didn't mean-' she pleaded, her words lost in the roar of the ocean. It was over in a moment; stickiness smearing her belly, thighs.

Orla curled herself into a ball, flinched when Pierre touched her shoulder. 'What's wrong, Ireland?' Everything, she wanted to scream, everything. How could she explain, she barely understood herself. She heard him root in his pockets, light a cigarette. He offered her one. Orla shook her head. She kept her back to him, absorbed in trying to animate the girl she'd encountered earlier, the one who'd braved the ocean. In the end she gave up, lay in a heap, not thinking. Pierre sat a little way off, smoking. The sea quietened and the faint thump of music seeped into her consciousness. She opened her eyes. In the distance, a rainbow of lights danced, blurry as though rain were falling. The music got louder then stopped abruptly, leaving only the sibilant hiss of waves.

The plane did a loop above the runway, doubling back as if allowing passengers one last look. Tumbling over one another, Sal and Kerry waved from a window seat to no one in particular. Orla, dressed in sensible homebound clothes, registered the swelling sea, the edging of lace on the white-hot sand. As the aircraft gained height, she noticed, for the first time, a line of jagged rocks jutting above the water like sentinels. She recalled the words on the brochure: paradise, it had promised.

Going Nowhere

Rod giggles. He imagines her coming out of the florist, arms full of fuckin' roses, shittin' herself when she sees the car's gone. Posh bitch, he thinks, running a hand over the soft upholstery. *Stupid* bitch, leaving the keys. He cuts into a stream of traffic. The car smells of perfume. He raises an arm, sniffs. A whiff of sweat and stale Lynx fill his nostrils. Not surprising, the day's stupid hot, the leather under his arse baking. He lowers a window, feels the wind warm on his face. A stranger grins at him from the side mirror: trackie top transformed into a smart jacket, white shirt open at the neck; around him it's all desert, air sweet and dry and up ahead a thousand miles of open road. Rod slows to cruise. Better be careful, cow like that will be onto the pigs pronto. He presses the CD button and a voice like a tyre bursting fills the car. Fuckin' opera! He pushes another knob, hears a woman explain something, earnest, fluttery, like Miss Hughes, one of the teachers at school. Not that she's taught him anything.

'What'ye think of the car Miss Shoes?' he bawls. 'Come a long fuckin way eh?' 'Bollix,' he adds wishing he could drive up there now, ram the fuckin' thing straight through the entrance, right into the class. Surprise the shite out of them.

Rod sheers onto the dual carriageway. He puts his foot down, swerves past a dozy Corsa, feels the car accelerate. 'Yaaahhhhh!!!' he screams, the tension that's been building all week exploding in his chest. 'Yaaaahhh!!!' He's never driven a BMW before. Pure fuckin' magic.

Rod slows. Time to dump it. Shame. He's grown fond of the car, doesn't like the thought of ramming it. Torch it? Asking for trouble in broad daylight. He racks his brains. His ma's right, he should go to school more often. What for? All he likes is cars and he's good at them, stealing and joy-riding since he was ten, as soon as his legs could reach the pedals. He's been lucky too, only done once and the shite judge let him off cos he'd no previous. Course his ma beat him sick to teach him a lesson. What does she know? Too many cars on the road, Jonesy says. Jonesy is Rod's hero. He's nineteen, has a licence. Who gives a fuck if his clothes stand up on their own; he breaths cars, lives them. Rod can depend on him. Most kids he knows are sniffin' or shootin', and older heads wouldn't spit on him, except to take the piss or get him to run messages. Jonesy's different. He has a job in a garage. Not some poxy kip that knows shag-all and sells sandwiches. *Heaney's* is dirtball territory with a pit deep and black as hell. Jonesy let him lie in it one day when the manager was off. "Think of it like a youngwan comin' down on ye" he'd joked, as a ton of metal descended. The manager likes Jonesy, lets him borrow cars. When he does, Jonesy has his own code: no speeding or letting Rod drive. Won't budge either. Rod respects that. Nicked cars are a different matter. Him and Jonesy have blown away quite a few: sent them to the giant scrap-yard in the sky. That's what Jonesy christened it. Not that Rod is like other joyriders, head-bangers only into riding cars to death, burning them. No appreciation. No. Cars eat up Rod's dreams; for him happiness is car-shaped. Fuck that, he thinks. What does it mean? Means he'll have to rob happiness or borrow it the rest of his life. No way he'll ever be able to afford a car like this. Fifty grand, more. Only one way to make that kind of money. His ma would skin him.

Rod raps on the wheel, stares out the window for inspiration. Along this stretch, the dual carriageway is thick with rows of low buildings, grey and ribbed like strips of dirty elastic. Legoland. His ma had a job in one of them until the company did a runner to Taiwan. Cheaper labour. He sees a sign for the Industrial Estate, cuts across the traffic. The buildings near the entrance are all smoked glass and revolving doors. After that its warehouses, most decorated with *TO LET* signs, then nothing, just mounds of earth and a couple of abandoned diggers. For something to do, he follows a line of placards with arrows painted on them before realising where they're taking him: Burke's Scrapyard. Fuck! Like he's been drawn there. Jimmy fuckin' Burke! Owes him for that hiding. Wouldn't believe it was heads from the Flats killed his fuckin' dog. Madman! Adrenaline ratchets as an idea forms in Rod's mind. Cool. Fuckin' cool. Pity Jonesy isn't here. He'd piss himself. The scrapyard, a huge metal sprawl, is on open ground at the arse end of the estate. Word on the street has it Burke had been holding out, hoping to make a killing with some American Corpo, only he left it too late. Another rumour is he's shitting himself in case someone comes along with a earth mover, uncovers a few missing parts the pigs have been looking for. Rod checks his mobile. It's near enough lunchtime. With any luck Burke and his henchmen will be holed up playing poker in the shack they call an office. Little shit-house on the prairie. The scrapyard's protected by a high fence, held together by pallets, panels, twists of barbed wire, probably electrified. Halfway along, he pulls over, opens the glove compartment. It's jammed with crap and he rummages through, finds a piece of paper, nothing written on it, a tube of lipstick. Perfect! He scribbles something, tosses it on the seat then, heart thumping like windscreen wipers, he noses towards the yawning corrugated gates. The blackened outline of a pit-bull salivates beneath a skull and cross-bones. Lower down, hand-painted letters bear the legend: Burke & Son, Scrap Metal Dealers. Dealers is right and it isn't only cars. Rod pulls up his hoodie, inches past the latest arrivals parked like rows of bad teeth. Behind them, towers of flattened cars sizzle in the heat like hamburgers. He holds his breath. If they catch him, they'll fuckin' mangle him. Easing out of the car, he zaps it, flings the keys into the nearest pile of junk. Growls erupt somewhere in the bowels of the yard. 'Good doggies,' he shouts, taking to his heels. At the gate, he looks over his shoulder, gloats at the shocking pink message: 'Happy Birthday Dickhead!' Rod giggles. Try explaining that to the pigs. Wanker!

Rod lets himself in. A familiar gloom douses his excitement, like someone pissing on a fire. Television noises leak from the living-room, bounce off grimy unpainted walls. He pushes in the door, sees his ma asleep on the couch, empty beer bottles on the floor. His half-sister Goldie doesn't look up. She's sitting in a halo of light that seeps through closed curtains.

'How'ye,' he says, hunkering beside the five year old.

The girl stops what she's doing, looks at him as if deciding whether she knows him. A gummy smile breaks her face in two. Silently, she hands him a square of brightly painted wood, motions him to add it to a pillar of blocks. Rod places it on top, his free hand hovering as the column sways. Goldie giggles, then with a swipe sends the whole thing toppling.

'What ye do that for?'

She shrugs, gathers up the blocks, starts again, her face serious, grown-up. Rod watches, hating the feeling that comes, like someone's using a tin opener on his chest. Just as suddenly another feeling replaces it and he wants to lash out, hit her.

He stands up, kicks one of the blocks.

'Want something to eat?'

Goldie nods, follows him to the kitchen.

Opening the fridge, he takes out an opened packet of cheese slices, the top ones hard, greasy. He throws those away, switches on the microwave, bungs in some half-thawed burger buns. Goldie clambers up, sits on the table peering into the lighted interior, hawing on the glass. Funny how they've got used to her not talking. The doctor said there was nothing wrong, she could speak if she wanted to. Rod likes her not talking. It's as if there's something pure about her, something untouched. It makes her special. He spreads marge on one of the buns, crams in some of the cheese. Goldie's his idea. Her real name's Kerry. He nicknamed her KerryGold after the butter, then Kerry got dropped and she became Gold, then Goldie. She bites into the bun he gives her, gobs it on the table, laughs.

'Dirty little bitch, don't do that!'

She squeezes another wodge between her gums.

'Don't!' he orders and she bows her head, swallows meekly.

'Why aren't you at school?' His ma's presence fills the kitchen.

'Let off early.' He offers her one of the buns.

37

She makes a face, flops into a chair. He can smell sour beer off her breath. 'Shut your mouth when ye eat,' she bawls at the girl.

'Leave her alone.'

'Sez who?'

Rod doesn't answer. His ears pick up the wail of a siren and he slouches across to the window.

'Yer pals comin' to collect ye?' his ma cracks, opening the fridge with her foot.

'Very funny.'

He hates her being there, wishes she'd go back to the living-room. If it wasn't for Goldie he'd find a squat.

'Something happening?'

'Yeah. There's a dog pissing against a tree. Wait - there's two of them - they're having a competition.'

'Jaze, the excitement.' She folds her arms. 'You're not to be mitching, d'ye hear?'

'Sez who?'

'Watch it! You're not too big for a clatter.'

'What's the point? Fuckin' teachers are headbangers.'

'The point is so you won't grow up to be a savage.'

'Too late Ma. Haven't ye noticed, we are savages. Look at the state of this kip. Look at you!'

His ma's eyes blaze then the heat goes out and they fill up.

Shit. He hates it worse when she cries. At the corner of his eye, he sees Goldie get up, go to the woman's side. His ma pushes her away.

'She's only-', He stops, noticing the skin above her wrist is mottled. 'What happened yer arm?'

'That bastard came looking for money.'

The bastard is Rod's da. On paper anyway. The git did a runner when Rod was seven, showed up again last year. Since then, he's been turning up regular, doped out or scrounging money, promising things that will never happen.

'What d'ye let him in for?'

'Try stoppin' him,' she snaps. 'Anyway, it's no fun sitting here all day with the zombie.'

'I told ye not to call her that.' He checks to see if Goldie's listening but she's gone somewhere, staring into the distance, mouth open, eyes glazed.

His ma slops across to the sink, pours a glass of water. Rod looks at her, realises where the beer came from.

'What ye starin' at?' Her tone softens. 'I'm gaspin'. Have ye a fag?'

'I don't smoke.'

'Jaze, did I teach ye nothin'?' She shrieks laughing. Rod joins in. Out of nowhere, one of their moments erupts, his ma stamping her feet, Rod drumming the table. Goldie joins in, banging a spoon. They keep it up, rise to a crescendo; tears streaming down his ma's face.

'Shut-up in there!' a voice roars through paper-thin walls. Fists hammer.

Rod catches his ma's eye.

'Fuck off!' they scream in unison.

Maybe real families are like this all the time, Rod thinks.

'Faster,' Rod roars.

Jonesy revs and the engine whines like someone's stuck a pole up its hole. They're booting along the dual carriageway, in and out of cars, scaring the shite out of drivers. Women are the best targets. Rod gives them the finger if they're good-looking, two if they're ugly. The bike suddenly farts, slows.

'Outta juice - got any dosh?'

Rod shakes his head.

He hops off, watches Jonesy wheel it to the side of the road. The bike's legit, belongs to a cousin of his who's inside.

'Dump it. See if we can pick up something.'

'No way Jose. If this is in good nick when he gets out, Tony'll see me right.'

'Take us hours to get home.'

'Fuck off then.'

Rod considers it, knows he won't.

Instead, he takes out papers, rolls a ciggy. Funny, the way he keeps it secret from his ma. None of her business. After he's had a few pulls, he places it between Jonesy's lips. Jonesy sucks, clouds of smoke coming out his nose like dirty exhaust fumes. He goes back to pushing, the rolly hanging from his bottom lip. After a while, Rod takes a turn, Jonesy skipping alongside, his forehead looming in and out of a side mirror. Bucketed by speeding cars, Rod stares into the mizzy greyness. All of a sudden, it feels right being out on a night like this, pushing a bike, being a man. He thinks of saying something, doesn't. Overhead, some of the clouds that have been threatening, make up their mind. Rain pours down, dances on the tarmac, on the gleaming metal. Rod curses, glances over at Jonesy.

'Ye look like a fuckin' drowned rat!'

They scream laughing.

An SUV passes, a couple of kids cosseted in the muggy interior. Rod sticks his tongue out. The kids press against the back window, make faces. Jonesy chases after the car, scratching at his balls, squealing like a demented monkey.

Back at Jonesy's they open a couple of cans, flick on the telly. On the screen a man in a penguin suit pulls a card from an envelope. He calls out a name and a skinny woman who looks like she forgot to put on her dress rushes on stage. The man hands her a small statuette. The light catches it, spangles. Tears run down the actress' face as she holds up the Golden Globe.

'They should give us one for nickin' cars,' Jonesy jokes.

Jonesy makes puking noises as the woman rattles on about everyone being there for her, especially her mother. The camera closes in on a dyed blonde in the audience.

'Fuck,' Rod says, remembering he promised to be home early, let his ma out for a drink. 'Gotta go.'

Last time he was late, she'd fucked off, leaving Goldie on her own. He'd found her, red-eyed, clinging to the banisters.

'Here, take one of these.' Joneys hands him a can.

Rod stuffs it in a pocket, heads back into the rain. By the time he reaches his road, he's wet through, dog-tired. He imagines himself in bed; the thought cheers him. He'll say he's sick in the morning; Goldie can stay home too, she's a new video game they can try. Turning into the estate, he sees the house is pitch dark. He kicks open the gate, fumbles in his jacket for a key.

'Fuckin' cunt!!' A fist collides with the side of his head. Dazed, Rod tries to steady himself but a second punch knocks him off his feet. He curls automatically, covering his head, anticipating the kick that explodes a second later like a crater opening in the middle of his back.

'Fuckin' .. bitch, lock me out me own house. Would ye!'

Recognising his da's spaced-out slur, Rod tries to speak but the sound gets strangled as another kick hits home.

'Teach ye .. teach ye .. cunt, bitch!' The voice begins to break up. He hears footsteps backing off, running. Then the pain takes over.

Rod stirs. He's lying in a pool of wet. So this is it, he thinks, surprised by a sudden, unexpected sense of relief. The thought crosses his mind that he'll never drive a car into the sunset and a smile creases his dirt, blood-spattered face. He puts a hand to the wetness, raises a finger, licks. It tastes of beer.

He finds his key, manages to open the door, collapses. When he comes to, Jonesy is shouting in his ear. He struggles up, tries to make a joke of it, feels ashamed when he cries. He wants his ma but she's not there. Jonesy rings a hackney. In casualty they take x-rays, tell him a bone in his cheek is fractured. An inch higher, he'd be brain-damaged, dead even. They keep him in for observation. Later, a nurse asks if he knows who did it. He doesn't answer. She tells him they've notified the police, that someone will be round to take a statement. No one comes. He drifts in and out of sleep, forgetting where he is each time he wakes up. The day drags on. Towards evening, he watches the nurses come and go, waits for the right moment to do a bunk. He hurts all over, like someone's stitched his body together with fishing tackle. He fixes his mind on home, on getting there. As he shuffles along, he wonders what time it is, what day, why his ma never showed up.

The house is stone empty but he walks round anyway, shouting 'Ma, Goldie,' louder and louder, slamming doors, kicking whatever gets in his way. From next door, a voice roars a warning. He scrambles across, pounds on the wall, screams curses. Exhausted, he crawls upstairs, falls into bed, the duvet over his head to block out the yellow glow of the streetlights. On the edge of sleep, he plots revenge.

Next morning, Rod wakes to a ringing in his head, realises it's the phone. He struggles out of bed, locates the sound in his ma's room.

He holds the receiver to his ear, says nothing.

'That you Rod?' his ma asks.

'Where the fuck are ye?' Tears come to his eyes; he has to stop himself throwing the handset across the room.

There's a silence.

He starts to tell her what happened.

'I know about the fuckin' bastard,' she interrupts, 'why d'ye think I'm not home? He came for me the other night. I'm black and blue.'

'I don't give a fuck.'

'I do. I had enough when you were young. Kerry's not going through it.'

'Her name's Goldie. Where are yous?'

'Somewhere safe.'

'Ma, don't. I'll stay in, I'll take care of Goldie, honest.'

He hears beeps.

'Put money in Ma.'

There's a rattle of coins and she swears as one gets stuck.

'I'm going t'see if I can get us re-housed. Rod you're old enough. I was pregnant at your age.'

He drops the phone, walks out of the room.

'Are ye there Rod?' she shouts but he's halfway down the stairs.

He misses Goldie. She's a point of light. Now there's none. He hangs round a house he knows battered women go to until an oulwan with an arm in a sling tells him to fuck off. He goes home, stares out a window. That night, he hauls a mattress into the sitting-room, drinks cider until he passes out. Next day he strips the kitchen, takes the stuff to the pawn. The man offers fifty for the lot, tells Rod he's lucky to catch him in a good mood. When Rod insists the microwave's worth a hundred, he gets nasty. Rod considers the tattoos decorating the man's biceps, takes the money. Outside, he knocks over a table of ornaments, runs off laughing. He lives on burgers and chips, feels tension mount. He needs a car.

Rod kicks a wheel.

'That bad?' Jonesy asks, emerging from under a bonnet.

He nods.

'Finish about seven. See ye in Macs?'

Rod says nothing, examines a greasy rag with his toe cap. Jonesy puts a hand in his overall, takes out a note.

'Pay ye back,' Rod swears, pocketing it.

Macs is jam-packed. Rod's underage, not that anyone gives a toss. This is three monkeys country: see nothing, hear nothing, do nothing. The barman stares over Rod's head as he orders a pint of cider. He sinks it, feels the liquid course through his bloodstream, adrenaline kick in. He orders another. Tonight's the night, he tells himself. He's buzzing when Jonesy arrives, anxious to go but they have a drink for luck, Rod blessing himself with froth. The Omniplex is two blocks away. They don't speak on the way, part of a ritual that's grown up between them. Automatically, they make for the car park at the rear. Three rows back they're in luck, an open window: half an inch but it's all they need. Jonesy looks at Rod. The car's a poxy Toyota. Rod shrugs. As Jonesy sets to work, Rod keeps lookout in case some dickhead decides to interfere. A door clicks in the darkness. Rod jumps in as the engine shudders to life.

'We'll swop over at the Hen,' Jonesy lays down the law.

'Ah fuck!'

Rod knows it's wise to wait but he's jumpy, itching to get his hands on the wheel.

'Wanta get us stopped?' Jonesy clips him round the ear, manoeuvres the car towards the exit. As they wait for a flood of traffic to clear, Rod finds 2FM, switches it to full volume. The car vibrates and he bounces up and down, hands drumming the dashboard. 'Move you fuckers!' he roars as an ancient Merc shoots from the line, levels with them. Rod's hand is poised for the one finger salute when he recognises the driver.

'It's Mad Burke!' he screams, 'Get out of here!'

Jonesy lurches onto the road. A Passat swerves, brakes. Angrily, the driver leans on the horn.

'Nothing else to play with, scabby bastard!' Rod roars out a window, checking to see if Burke has copped them. In the darkness, tail lights circle the car park, U-turn.

'Boot it,' he squeals, 'he's after us.'

'What the fuck are you on about?' Jonesy demands.

Rod tells him about the BMW.

'How would he know it was you, fucksake.'

At the lights the Passat draws up beside them. 'That was dangerous driving back there,' the driver roars, 'hoodlums like you shouldn't be allowed on the road. Kill yourself and everyone else.'

'Fuck you,' Rod exults as they tear away. 'Toe rag!'

They hang a left, leave the main drag, Rod popping to the music. Jonesy's right. Stupid getting worked up over a bollix like Burke. Couldn't pin anything on him anyway. He settles back, tunes into a feeling he's having, a feeling something's going to happen. Hums to it. The Toyota swings into an alleyway, a short-cut for delivery vans, cuts back into the traffic near the intersection for the motorway.

A short distance ahead the *R* and *E* of Red Hen blink on and off. Jonesy drives in, parks.

'She's all yours.'

Rod leaps out, laughing as Jonesy pretends to do himself an injury on the gear stick. 'Any word from your ma?' he asks, starting on a rolly.

'Fuck her.'

Rod narrows his eyes, puts his foot down. Tyres spark as the car hurtles towards a gap in the traffic.

'Jeesus fuck!! What are ye-!' Jonesy wrenches the wheel. 'Tryin' to get us killed! Pull the fuck over if you're gonna drive like that.'

'Fuck off,' Rod answers but does what he's told.

Jonesy sucks on his cigarette.

'You're fuckin mad you are.'

'And you're chicken.'

Jonesy blows a smoke ring.

'I said you're chicken.'

A vein in Jonesy's temple beings to throb. He opens the car door.

'I'm waiting.'

'Fuckin' wait then.'

Jonesy flicks the butt into the darkness, steps out after it.

Rod guns the car, doesn't look back. Jonesy was outta line bringing up his ma. He doesn't want to think about her. Doesn't want to think about anything. What's there to think about? Tonight's the night, he repeats over and over and a wall of darkness that's at the edge of his mind, a wall he's been driving towards for years, blazes. This is what he's been living for. The rest can fuck. As his foot finds the accelerator the machine wraps itself round him like a glove and he feels the pull taking his breath, his body, his whole mind. The car glides as if on ice, speed enveloping him until he merges with the engine, the metal, feels he is speed, chewing up the road as it flashes towards him. Headlights appear. He puts his foot down. Harder. The headlights blur, crowd in on him, glowing. Glowing, like gorgeous golden globes.

Things We Need To Remember

'**W**hat on earth could Fiona want to talk to you about? You haven't seen each other in years.' I shrug. The letter, out of the blue, is as much a mystery to me.

'She is my cousin,' I protest.

'Oh, for goodness sake!' Mummy retorts. 'Let me see it.'

Fiona is from the wrong side of the family. My father's. Mummy and Daddy divorced when I was young. We never talk about it. Mummy's a real snob so I've always assumed it had something to do with my father coming from farming stock. Acres of boggy land; but no doctors, solicitors, no one of importance. Nothing only a farm beneath a hill. I study my mother as she trawls through the illegible writing; marvel at the pretensions of small towns. She's dressed in tennis whites, her latest craze. The game itself will be a short one, a preamble to drinks, a chance to show off her trim legs, tanned and healthy. Gleaming. Like her hair, her nails, her smile.

'Drop a polite note, tell her you can't come, there's a darling.' She eyes the clock, scowling in a careful, poised way, a way that doesn't invite wrinkles. 'Where *is* Nora?'

'Maybe I will go,' I say, mainly to annoy her.

'You can't. You haven't-,' she breaks off, crosses to the bay window and waves. By the purse of her lips, I know Nora's driving the 4-wheel, not the BMW. Fixing a smile in place, mummy strides out, humming something from Gilbert & Sullivan. I watch her kiss-kiss Nora, then I slump down in an armchair. I'm twenty-two, an only child. In less than a month I'm leaving for Australia. For good. In my imagination Australia's one big empty space, easy to get lost in, a place where the air doesn't belong to anyone, where everything doesn't have a price tag. Or maybe it's just the other side of the world. Re-reading the letter, I'm suddenly catapulted back to a pale, humid, summer morning. Fiona, finger to her lips, is leading me to where a hen is laying wild. Reaching the spot, she scatters the bird, urges me to pick up the eggs. They're warm, festooned with feathers, specks of shit. Our eyes meet over our find, sparkle. I loved my older cousin, even though she wore old-fashioned clothes, smelled a bit. She alone made up for the fact I was shunted off to the wilds of Connemara each year while Mummy and Daddy went God knows where. The visits stopped when I was thirteen, the year they separated. For a while, Fiona and I exchanged Christmas cards, but eventually they petered out. Mummy's right of course, a visit now would be inconvenient; all the same I'm intrigued, flattered in a strange way. Fiona was only two years older but I always saw her as wise beyond her years. She taught me to smoke, she even taught me the facts of life, country-style: "Ye wanta see the young bulls at it like, they'd jump on anythin'. C'mon I'll show ye."

Besides, if things were to go disastrously wrong there was always Iseult's. Iseult is a friend from University. She's had no luck getting a job, is dying of boredom on the family farm near Clifden according to her latest e-mail. Going would also have the advantage of cutting short the endless socialising and shopping Mummy's planning, her way of stemming guilt. At Fiona's I'd be out of reach, I reflect, pocketing the letter.

A dog barks loudly as I drive in. I park, roll down the window, hoping the noise will bring someone to the front door which is wide open. The dog, an old collie, stretches and shakes its head, then after a desultory once-over, goes back to sleep. The place itself looks like it's been sleeping for years. The house is smaller, dingier, like an old photograph that's lost its colour. I seem to remember window boxes spilling with petunias but there are no signs of any. There are no flowers at all. It flashes through my mind that Fiona's mother died a few years ago - Mummy sent a wreath - and I try to summon up an image of my aunt but all that comes to mind is a stained housecoat, a pair of work-worn hands.

'Hel-lo,' I call, getting out.

An untidy looking woman emerges, blinks in the sunlight.

'Niamh, it's you! Thought it was Robert about turf.'

Neither of us move. I see her take in the car, clothes, the new hair-do. I can almost hear her thinking she's made a terrible mistake.

'Daddy won't be back for a while. Come in, come in, you'll take a cup of tea or something.'

I'd like something, something strong, but I don't think that's what she means.

'Thanks,' I say. 'Will I bring my stuff?'

'Ah, leave it 'til later. We can have a chat.'

I step carefully across the dung-spattered yard, my town shoes thin and out of place.

In the kitchen, Fiona potters round in an unorganised fashion, while I sit uncomfortably in a hard chair. The room's in shadow, the red Sacred Heart lamp giving off an eerie glow. It's impossible not to see the place through Mummy's eyes, hear her critical voice in my ear. As my cousin sets about making tea in a grimy teapot, she questions me about the journey: was it as far as I remembered; did I think things had changed? I tell her I had to ask for directions in the village, but that now I'm here it all seems familiar. We make more small talk and I drink my tea too quickly, burn my tongue. I say nothing and we smile politely over the rims of our cups like children playing at being grown-ups.

Mummy was right, I think, this isn't going to work. Best get it over with, drive to Iseult's first thing in the morning.

'You said you wanted to talk about something? Your letter.'

Fiona feels in a pocket, produces a pack of cigarettes. 'D'ye still smoke? You were a divil for them when you use come. D'ye remember we'd sit in the loft, puffing away?'

'I never really liked them. Mummy smokes.'

A door opens in her eyes, shuts. Too late, I remember her mother died from cancer.

'Better off. Bad for ye,' she says, inhaling deeply. 'The thing is ... I want to leave, get away from this dump. It's ... well, since Mammy died, ... I was the only one left ... so I had to, like, take over. Daddy wasn't too bad then. The others came home, once in a while, help with the harvest but now not one of them even sends a postcard. They all fell out with him like so it's on my shoulders.'

I nod, wonder if she's heard I'm going to Australia.

The buzz of a tractor fills the room.

Fiona's eyes stare out the open door, she twists the cup in her hand. There's a silence and I become aware of a strong odour pervading the room, cloying. Following her gaze, I notice the lane's clotted with May blossom.

'D'ye think you could talk to him, convince him like - for me to leave? Will ye? Will ye try? Promise,' she hisses, then turns her back as my uncle strides in.

'Well, well, you answered the summons, Miss Conneely.' Uncle Sean stands in the doorway, casting a shadow across the room. His remark is meant to be jokey but there's an edge and a knowing look on his face that makes me feel like an awkward teenager. I nod, smile, remember he used to frighten me: it was his way of saying things, letting you know he knew what you were thinking, that he was wise to your game.

'We're honoured. I hope this daughter of mine's been looking after ye.' From the tone of his voice it's obvious he couldn't give a damn. The tone changes. 'Is the dinner ready?' he barks.

'In the oven,' Fiona answers.

'I suppose we'll be spreading a tablecloth. How's your mother? Not that we were ever good enough for the likes of her.'

'Daddy!'

'Mummy's fine. She sends her regards.'

'Regards! She didn't have much regard for my brother. Airs and graces,' he mutters, running a hand over his stubbly chin. 'I think I'll have a wash and shave first. What do you think, Miss Conneely, would that be the proper thing to do?' ' Is there a clean shirt?' he adds.

Fiona rushes to get one and she's hardly out the door when he rounds on me, raising an eyebrow in her direction. 'Don't be putting ideas in her head, do I make myself clear?'

I open my mouth to remind him that it was Fiona who invited me but the words stick in my throat.

'Here you are.' Fiona tosses him an ironed shirt.

With a snort, he plods from the room.

Tears fill my cousin's eyes.

'What's wrong?' I ask.

Ignoring my question, she crosses the room, wiping her face with the back of her hand. 'Those bloody cows are out again.'

She pushes past and I follow, thinking how ridiculous this whole business is; I barely know these people.

In the yard, Fiona attempts to head off a large brown and white cow, blocking its path as it trundles towards her, udders heavy with milk. The animal squares up and there's a stand off before it turns away, scrambles back over a ditch of broken branches. I lend a hand mending the makeshift fence, dragging scattered branches, piling them on top of each other, trying not to snag my tights.

'Before Mammy died ... I was his pet, the one who got away with things, suppose I was youngest. Then he changed ... it was like he couldn't stand me. He'd get angry, shout-

'Won't he be finished by now?' I interrupt, not wanting to be dragged into their family squabbles.

'Rosie died, poor little Rosie.'

'Rosie?'

'My dog. A little toy poodle. I won her at a fair. Hated her, didn't he? Threw things at her if she came near. Useless bloody thing, he called her. Dunno, think like she frightened somethin' in him.' Her face softens. 'It use sleep on my bed.'

'Fiona!' A voice roars.

She looks towards the house. 'Poisoned! If I thought for one minute he-'

Tears glint, then with a shake of the head, she transforms herself.

'Comin', she roars back, 'cows out again.'

There's the rest of the evening to get through and I find myself missing home, even Mummy's forced chatter. The hands of the clock barely move and I wonder how long I need sit before I can make some excuse. Uncle Sean's engrossed in something called *The Farming Journal* which he rattles every now and then in a vaguely threatening way. Fiona's renovating a dress, something I thought had gone out with the Ark. I begin to see what Iseult was getting at in her email. I close my eyes, listen to the cows outside moaning and bellowing, as if they're in pain. At some point, Fiona looks up. 'Don't mind the noise of the crayturs. They're taking the calves tomorrow for slaughter. It's always the same. It's like they know.'

Next morning when I stumble down, Fiona's dressed to go out. 'Just running down to the village,' she announces, 'signing-on day.'

'I'll give you a lift,' I mumble. 'Give me a few minutes.'

'Sure there's no need. I enjoy the cycle. Help yourself, ' she says pointing to a packet of cereal.

Before leaving, she throws me a beseeching glance then nods towards her father who's searching for something in an overflowing cupboard. I pour a bowl of cornflakes, trying to recall the speech I rehearsed before falling asleep. The previous night it had my Uncle Sean on his knees, this morning it seems silly, pretentious. I make up my mind to wait until he finishes what he's doing, wing it. I study his back, the folds of flesh where the shirt eats into his neck, feel suddenly light-headed. Out of nowhere, an image flashes into my mind, like the fragment of a dream. It vanishes when I try to grab hold of it. My knuckles tighten.

Uncle Sean exclaims loudly, holds up a roll of thin cable. For a split second, I have the weirdest feeling it's going to attach itself to me, pull me across the room towards him.

'C'mon, ye might as well make yourself useful while yer here,' he grunts.

Without a murmur, I follow. There's a burning sensation in my spine as if it's melting. Outside, the cows continue the same mournful racket. Uncle Sean shifts impatiently in the yard. 'Make sure they don't escape the far side while I hitch this up.' He directs me where to stand. 'Clever crayturs. Sniff out a weak spot.' His eyes narrow. 'Humans do it too. It's only natural, I suppose.' Disdainfully, he prods the branches Fiona and I stacked. 'Stay put,' he orders. 'As soon as they see me they'll be over with their tongues hanging out, thinking I'm bringing something to ate.'

The field is muddy in patches, the grass cropped close to the ground.

'They'd never stop ating if you let them,' he says, bending to pick up a pole. 'No point spoiling them, they need a firm hand, otherwise they might get ideas.'

Like me, he means.

'Her dog died,' I hear myself saying as if we've been talking about Fiona all along.

'That yoke,' he spits, 'she was destroying it, making a bloody pet out of it, feeding it sweets and what have ye. Hated me it did, the little bastard. Snap and growl if it saw me coming. I put a- ' He stops, flushes red. 'Better off dead, useless feckin' thing.'

He whacks the pole in place, drops the hammer. 'She's not laving,' he adds as if talking to the air. 'I need her. When I'm carried out feet first she can go wherever the hell she pleases. Sell up for all I care.'

The cows shuffle over, mooing like their hearts are breaking. A few jostle, pawing at the branches, try to hoist themselves over.

'Catch this,' he calls, throwing the cable. While I hold it he walks backwards, unwinding as he goes. I stand there, feeling foolish, letting him get the better of me, knowing he can see right through me.

'A few volts will stop them in their tracks, eh?'

Fiona goes pale when I tell her what Uncle Sean said. He's gone with the calves and the two of us are alone, drinking one of the interminable cups of tea Fiona makes. I decide to leave out the bit about Rosie but I embroider the rest, making out I put up more of a fight than I did.

'I'll drop you to a train station, if you like?' I offer. I should ask her to come with me; this is a compromise.

Fiona lights a cigarette. Shrugs. Part of me wants to shake her, ask why she needs his permission.

Later, while I'm packing, she sticks her head round the door. 'Stay for lunch, why don't ye? Daddy will be home soon.'

'No. I need to get ...'

Our eyes meet.

'Good of you to come like ... all this way.'

I nod.

'It was good to see you.'

She stares at the ground a moment before hurrying away.

As I get into the car, I notice the cows are silent.

At a petrol station twenty miles away I reverse. If my cousin doesn't do something soon, it'll be too late. On the way back I berate myself for not having told her what Uncle Sean said about the poodle. The place seems changed when I get there as if it has closed back in on itself, my visit obliterated. At the sight of the jeep in the yard, my resolve weakens. What right do I have to disturb any of this? Resisting an urge to drive straight out, I turn off the engine, recite a list of Fiona's grievances to galvanise my courage. As usual, the front door is open. This time the collie doesn't even look up as I stand at the threshold, peer in. Fiona and her father are sitting at the table. I watch as she passes him a bowl of potatoes. From nowhere, a tiny dog leaps up, yapping and barking. I cry out in surprise and the pair glance up from their meal. Uncle Sean's face darkens. 'Down,' he commands the puppy. Our eyes meet. 'Back so soon?' he says in a mocking voice.

'We're having a bit of lunch, would you like some?' Fiona asks in an embarrassed, half-hearted way.

I look from one to the other, swallow. 'I think I left something-' I disappear into the bedroom, pretend to search; hover by the door for what seems an eternity.

'Must be in my case,' I say coming out.

Fiona stands up. 'D'ye see what Daddy bought me?' She points to the basket where the dog has retreated.

I nod.

'We'll put manners on this one,' Uncle Sean says. 'Breeding goes a long way, you know.'

Out of sight of the house I pull over, allow the tears flow. The heady perfume of the May seeps in through an open window. I stare out at it, remember reading it's considered unlucky to bring it into the house. The blossoms blur as an image unfurls: a man's back, folds of flesh eating into a shirt, a woman beneath him. As I watch, the figure tries to struggle out from under but the man pins her down. 'You're my wife,' my father screams, 'act like one.'

'Mummy,' I cry from the doorway. 'Mummy.'

My mother's face rears, red, tear-streaked. 'Get out,' she screams. 'Get out of here!'

Back home, I sit in the driveway, my eyes fixed on the smooth tarmacadem, the symmetrically arranged flowerbeds, the pollarded trees.

'Mummy,' I call, stepping into the hallway.

'In here, darling.'

She's stretched on a sofa, circles of cucumber on both eyelids. I stare at her and she wriggles her toes.

'You're back early. How were the Barbarians?'

'They were- Mummy, we have to talk.'

She peals off a piece of cucumber, squints at me.

'Of course, of course. Not now though!'

'About you and Daddy,' I hurry on.

She crosses to a mirror, stares into it. 'I don't think it makes the slightest bit of difference. What do you think? Do I look all wide-eyed?' Her voice is coy, childlike.

'Mummy, are you listening?'

'Yes darling but it'll have to wait. Saturday's my bridge-

'Cancel it.'

Her face hardens.

'I can't cancel a bridge game just like that.'

I hand her the mobile. 'Yes you can Mummy,' I tell her, 'you can.'

The Chemist's Assistant

It's 1961 and the first man's just walked in Space but where I live it might as well be the Dark Ages. You won't believe this but my father keeps a cane hanging on the wall. On one side of the room is a picture of the Sacred Heart with eyes that follow you everywhere and on the other side, the cane. Like a big question mark saying: what have you done? My friend Maudie says it's corporal punishment and someone should report him. Everyone's afraid of my father. Even my big sister Anne and she's his pet. I'm still sore from last night. I know I shouldn't have robbed the money but it was only sixpence. I don't really remember taking it but I can remember buying Nancy Balls.

That's why I'm sitting on a wall on a Saturday instead of being at the Pictures. I didn't get any pocket money cos of stealing. I love the Pictures, especially ones with women in them. War films or films about submarines are boring. Horror's all right although they always make the woman do something stupid, like, if there's a vampire on the loose she has to go for a walk on her own exactly where he's lurking. D'ye ever notice that? Course that way the hero can come along in the nick of time and rescue her. It never happens the other way round. And the women who get rescued are always beautiful. Plain ones are goners, you can count on that. It's hard to believe women can be that beautiful. Like Goddesses. The women round here are run-down looking except for Angela, who used to live opposite the chemist shop. She had this long golden hair, wavy, that hung over her face. Probably bleached, but she looked like an angel. My mother and the woman-across-the-road were always giving out about her. Whenever she'd click-clack past on stilettos they'd shake their heads, make tight purses of their lips. Jealous, you could tell. No wonder Angela moved. Here's Mammy now and the woman-across-the-road back from shopping. Yap, yap, yap, they're so engrossed they stop right in front of me like I'm not there.

'Have you seen the new arrival at the chemist?' the woman-across-the-road asks, her voice all mysterious.

Mammy's eyes widen and she nods 'yes'. Then she notices me.

'What are ye sitting on the wall for?'

'I'm not,' I say, hopping off.

There's nothing to do so I decide to go down the chemist, see what they're talking about. Grumpy, the man who runs it, hates kids, shouts if you touch anything, as if touching's any harm. He knows me though because I go there all the time to collect prescriptions. Did I tell you my mother's always ill? Nobody knows what's wrong with her but my Auntie says it all started when my brother was born dead. That was before I was born so I don't know. I never mind going to the chemist, the smell is gorgeous. Perfume and powder. It's full of things too. On the counter there's rows of plastic nails, painted, and fake lipsticks with real ones underneath. But it's the bottles of perfume I love. There's loads, different colours too, green, red, frosted, some have stoppers like eyedroppers only fancier with snakes or hearts carved on them. I'm going to buy every one of them when I grow up.

When I walk into the chemist, I nearly drop dead. Behind the counter there's a new man in a white coat. But that isn't it. He's black! I've never seen a black person except in films. And here's one. In the flesh. He smiles at me. His eyeballs are really white just like in films. Grumpy shuffles around, kind of embarrassed.

'What's your name?' the black man asks.

I'm not sure he means me so I say nothing.

'I am Mussola.' He points to himself like I haven't understood the question. I want to tell him I'm just surprised, that adults here don't go

56

round being polite or introducing themselves. I look at Grumpy to see what he makes of it but he's busy shoving rolls of film into envelopes.

'Lecky,' I smile back, adding 'Colette.'

When he holds out his hand, I keep mine in my pocket.

'Don't you shake hands in this country?'

'Only if you're older.' I try not to stare but his hand is amazing, the inside pink with black lines where the creases are. His lips are the same. Black on the lip part then fading to pink where the skin goes into his mouth.

Mussola laughs, a loud, booming laugh.

'You look like you never seen a black man before.'

I feel myself go red as a beetroot and run out of the shop.

It's by accident I find out Mussola's on his own there Wednesdays. I'm playing outside and my mother comes out, says I've to take some stale bread back to Grennans. I hate having to do that. She's the one buy's the bread; I don't know why she can't take it back. Grennans is next to the chemist and Wednesday is Grumpy's half-day so it's a bit of a surprise to see the shop open. I peer over the window display, see Mussola filling shelves. I'm about to head off when he notices me, waves me in.

'How are you today Colette?'

I shrug.

'I like to practice my English,' Mussola explains. He imitates my shrug. 'No good.'

He laughs his big friendly laugh and I join in. He shrugs several times and I almost wet my knickers.

'Your English is really good,' I tell him. 'Is that what you're here for, to learn?'

'I am studying to be a pharmacist,' he tells me.

'What's that?'

'A chemist.'

'Oh.'

'In my country we need chemists, doctors, that class of person.'

I nod, noticing some new lipsticks have come in. The phone rings and Mussola excuses himself.

Luscious Colours for Summer, the ad for the lipstick says.

When I wave goodbye, he's still on the phone.

That night I put my hand in my pocket, find one of the lipsticks. I can't figure out how it got there. Then I hear sugar and spice Anne creaking across from the bathroom so I stick it in behind the wardrobe. I'll put it back next Wednesday when Mussola's not looking, I decide.

I begin to drop down every Wednesday. Mussola likes me to. He tells me that not many people talk to him so his English isn't improving. I try to teach him slang like 'get up the yard' and 'you're a right eigit' but they sound different when he says them. I like the way they sound, so Mussola says them over and over just to make me laugh. He tells me I'm his best friend.

Every week I add something new to my collection, perfume, a bottle of hand cream, even a set of emery boards, whatever they are. Mussola says when I'm older I can come and visit where he lives, meet the rest of his family. He says the sun shines there all the time and I'll be able to swim every day. I don't tell him I can't swim because maybe I'll learn. I think my mother is getting suspicious. She told me I'm not to be hanging round the chemist shop, that people have work to do and I'm only annoying them. What did I tell ye, she's jealous of everyone I like.

'Go and get this,' my father orders, handing me a prescription as soon as I put my school bag down. 'And come straight back.'

The doctor had to come to the house today and my father's off work so my mother must be really sick. I hate going to the chemist when Grumpy's there because Mussola and me can't talk. Grumpy keeps an eye on him, tells him off later for wasting time. That's what Mussola said. Said he wouldn't stick it but he's no choice. I've never heard an adult say that. Adults I know have all the choices.

I play not walking on lines as I go down the road. Now my mother's sick I'll probably have to do all the housework. Goody-goody Anne's studying for the Inter and is let off everything. It's not fair. When I get as far as Maudie's, I stop; I can see her head through the window. She makes a face when she sees me then her mother appears and gives me one of her 'clear off' looks. I glance down, see I'm standing on a line.

That's bad luck, I think, then I remember my da's waiting and hurry off. I nearly faint when I see a police car parked outside the chemist. Inside, a guard is talking to Grumpy and Mussola. Keeping one eye on the shop, I pretend to look into a garden as if I'm admiring the flowers. A few minutes pass then all of them come out and get into the car. I close my eyes so they don't see me. When I open them the car's gone. I wait ages and it's only after a while I realise the garden I'm looking into belongs to the house where Angela used to live. I remember how beautiful she was; wonder where she is now.

My father curses when I tell him the chemist is shut. I don't mention the police in case my voice gives anything away. Still grumbling, he puts on his coat, says he'll have to go to another chemist miles away and I'm not to move, in case my mother calls. I nearly say Anne's home but I don't. When he's gone, I mope round wondering what to do. What if they've arrested Mussola for stealing? It'll be my fault if he's put in prison. I put the catch on the bedroom door, feel behind the wardrobe, half-hoping I imagined the whole thing. But it's all there. I sit on the bed, thinking. I know what I should do. I should take everything down to the police station and prove Mussola's innocence, just like they do in films. I lie back, see Mussola's face light up when they set him free. I begin to feel all warm and glowy. That must be how the hero feels when he rescues the woman.

After I gather up the stuff, I tiptoe into my mother's bedroom, make sure she's asleep. Then I creep downstairs so as not to wake her. Anne's in the front room, her nose stuck in a book.

'Tell Daddy I had to go round to Maudie's. I forgot to take down some homework. And listen out for Mammy.' She barely looks up. Bloody swot!

Outside, I hurry for a bit, excited almost, then slow down as I get near the police station. What if they put *me* in jail? Jail! That's nothing to what my father will do when he finds out. And everyone will know I'm a robber. All the same, I can't let Mussola take the blame. He's my friend. The only grown-up who asks me questions, listens to what I say. Walking in through the gates of the station, I stick my hands in my pockets, feel the lipstick's smooth case, the glassy coldness of a perfume bottle. In films things always turn out OK.

'Lecky! What are you doing here?'

I blink, see Mussola standing in front of me.

'You escaped!'

'Escaped? Whatever are you talking about?'

'The police. I saw them taking you away.'

He laughs. 'Oh that. It was a technicality. About my papers. There were some forms to be signed. But why are you here?'

'Nothing.' I shrug, kicking at the ground.

He imitates the shrug but I can't seem to laugh. We stand a moment, each of us looking in opposite directions.

'See you tomorrow,' he says. 'It's Wednesday, don't forget.'

'I can't.' I'm about to make up something when I realise I can tell the truth. 'My mother's ill so I'll have to stay home.'

'Your mother is a lucky woman. Very lucky.'

I screw up my eyes. 'What d'ye mean?'

'You are ...' He scratches his head. 'Fishing for the compliments.'

I blush. 'No, honest, I'm not.'

'Colette ... Colette. If I have a daughter, I hope she will be just like you.'

I see he means it, go all wobbly.

'Have to go. My da will kill me.'

'See you later alligator,' he shouts.

'In a while crocodile,' I answer but I don't look back.

The End Of The Game

Brother Stanislaus' new soles echoed as he paced the ornate Italian floor in the large, empty hall that had once been a ballroom. The sound intruded on his prayers. Glancing down, he registered the deeply indented creases on the uppers of his shoes. The shoemaker might have given them a new lease of life but were they good enough for the ceremony? The last thing he wanted was to embarrass his mother. Perhaps he should have a word with Brother Superior about getting another pair. Not that temporal things mattered. Not at all. In reality, he was the one getting a new lease of life: taking his final vows, entering fully the life of the Community, the life of Christ. At the thought, the young man's body shrank and he sought diversion in the arabesque of snakes beneath his feet. Today the writhing creatures seemed to mock him: their incessant circular dance mimicking the endless thoughts circling his brain. Annoyed at being so easily distracted, Stanislaus returned to his novena. But he couldn't concentrate. Dizzy, he stumbled towards one of the upright chairs lining the walls, sat, took his head between large callused hands. Everyone had second thoughts he consoled himself, that was normal. Hadn't Brother Jarlath sent a personal letter to each seminarian suggesting they come and talk over any doubts. The final renunciation, the final letting go was a big step. Stanislaus gazed at the dun-coloured walls surrounding him. The caked paint had bubbled and cracked over the years, showing patches of white that reminded him of snow. A mountain appeared in his mind's eye, ghostly, soul-white and a sudden urge to scrape away the rest of the paint, to escape to the pristine pureness of just such a landscape overwhelmed him. There he could do battle with the elements, engage with something physical, tangible, let go of this unending struggle with spirit. 'Satan, behind me', Stanislaus muttered. Mollycoddling, staying indoors on account of a bit of frost was at the root of this. Air was what he needed, a blast of God's cold air would knock the rot from his mind.

Stanislaus opened the heavy outer door, stepped outside. A blanket of snow covered the Dublin Mountains visible in the distance. Smiling at God's irony, he took out his breviary. Within minutes, it was back in the pocket of his soutane. "Pick up your cross and follow Me", Christ had said. Stanislaus had answered the call, now he felt the full weight of that cross on his shoulders. The young man swallowed. Maybe it was time to pay a visit to Brother Jarlath. "Even Our Lord had doubts," the older man had warned. "At a time like this you'll be plagued: about the life you're turning your back on, the strength of your vocation, your own worthiness. Temptation will come, the way it came to our Saviour in the desert. The Devil will be at your side, waiting, watching, enticing." Stanislaus shut out his Superior's voice. What advice could Brother Jarlath give him? Prayer? He'd tried that. Mortification? He eat only what others put in front of him and at night forced himself out of bed, kneeling upright for long periods while others slept. The advice he wanted, the advice he longed to hear, he dared not - could not - hope for. Last minute nerves, he told himself, walking fast in a bid to outstrip his thoughts. But his thoughts kept pace, refusing to be pacified. Stanislaus slowed down. A spot of physical work would do the trick.

Gerry Raftery, as Brother Stanislaus had once been called, was no stranger to hard work. Growing up on a stony farm it had been as natural as breathing. Until the day of his tenth birthday, the day he'd out-paced his older brother making haycocks, he'd never even questioned it. "I'm King of the Castle," Gerry had roared from the top of a rick, "you're the dirty wee rascal!" Joe had stared up at him, a strange smile curling his lip. "That's what you think! Don't matter what you do, ye know, it's me'll get the farm. I'm the eldest." The words had hit Gerry like a thunderbolt. Brooding on them, things had fallen into place: the special treatment meted out to Joe by his father: taking him to the Mart, kneeling beside him at Mass. Gerry had felt betrayed, as if he didn't count. He'd racked his brain for some way of getting his father's attention, of proving his worth. Eventually, he'd hit on the idea of becoming an altar boy even though it meant missing football for christenings or weddings, even worse, getting slagged by his classmates. The plan had paid off. "That's my lad serving, him and Fr. Sheehy are like that," Mr Raftery would remark, crossing two fingers and winking at neighbours as they huddled outside the church gates after Mass, exchanging prices, football scores. "We'll make a priest of ye yet," he'd gloated another time over Sunday dinner. "Ye have to have money for that," his mother had snapped, rubbing two fingers together, a totally different meaning. Ladling out potatoes, she'd gazed lovingly at her favourite. "Don't be putting ideas in the lad's head. He has enough already."

But the germ had taken root and when a pair of Christian Brothers came on a recruiting mission to the school, Gerry had been the first to put his name down. That evening he'd seen his father's chest plump with pride. Three months later he'd packed his suitcase. He was thirteen.

"I put aside childish things." The words came to Stanislaus, as, spade in hand, he emerged from the dank gardening shed into daylight. That was the sacrifice required of every boy entering St Jude's. Of course there were games, Gaelic, hurling and on feast days, monopoly and scrabble were permitted; all the same it was as if a wand had been waved and childhood had disappeared. Passing the windows of the refectory, Stanislaus' attention was caught by gleaming white tablecloths. How he'd dreamed of his mother's cooking during those early months, of her apple tarts and rhubarb pies, the blackberry jam she made each September. At Jude's there were no favourites, no second helpings. He'd never have survived if it hadn't been for the evening rambles organised by Brother Ambrose. The elderly brother, dead now, had used the outings to demonstrate God's mysterious ways but he was passionate about birds and his passion had rubbed off on the younger boys, easing their lot. Eagerly, the fledgling bird-watchers had passed the one pair of binoculars between them as they attempted to identify choughs and lapwings or the swift flying wheatears with their give-away white, like a flash of snow in summer.

Turning into the kitchen garden, Stanislaus saw that the lazy beds were laced with frost, the ground hard. All the better, he thought, plunging in the spade, meeting resistance with force. From a nearby tree, a grating rattle startled him. Glancing up, he saw a lone magpie. What was it his mother used say? *One for sorrow* ... The bird took flight and Gerry kept it in his line of vision, watching it getting smaller and smaller, until finally he couldn't see it. A moment later, another bird or maybe the same one flew into sight. *Two for joy* ... Stanislaus sighed as the spade hit rock. Sometimes, it felt as though it wasn't just his childhood that had vanished but a part of him, or maybe all of him, and another person, someone who called himself Brother Stanislaus had taken his place. As he bent to remove several earth-clogged stones, Stanislaus felt the coldness of the soil. It was during that first terrible year the transformation had begun. The real him, the one he'd eventually had to let go of, appeared only at night, yearning for his mother, missing her, missing his father too, his brothers and sisters, the farm, the outhouses, the cowboys and indians he kept in a box under his bed. Everything from his past, even insignificant things, seemed to have the power to wrench his heart from his breast. He could remember lying awake, an apple tree or a clump of weeds hoared by winter frost taking on a magical appearance, calling to him. And the ache - so terrible at times he thought he'd die. Family visits had been a nightmare. Then he'd been forced to keep up a bright chatter, avoid his mother's eyes, aware of her dismay at the cold, comfortless sitting-room, tears threatening as she kissed him, her hand pressing his too tightly. And the time Josie, his favourite sister, had asked - their father out of earshot - if he was happy, if he wanted to come home? Concealing the lump in his throat, he'd muttered about having a vocation and she'd almost tumbled him: "That doesn't sound like you talking. Have they given you a brain transplant or what?" Once or twice during those visits, he'd been on the verge of blurting out his mistake, but the respect he'd heard in his father's voice when speaking to the other Brothers, the way he'd looked at Gerry and saw 'Brother Stanislaus' had steeled him and he'd said nothing. Tossing the last of the stones into a small pile, Stanislaus leaned on his spade: this sort of thinking was no help. It wasn't as if his superiors hadn't been aware of what he was going through. They knew all about severing the umbilical cord; the Order had its own way of dealing with it. Hard work, discipline, repetition: each day repeating itself, each a mirror of the previous, of the one to come, until they melted one into the other, became months, years; until finally it was hard to remember what life had been like outside, harder still to imagine venturing out. As places went, Jude's had a reputation for being soft – Brother Jarlath was one of the youngest Superiors, considered modern. From time to time, Stanislaus had heard rumours of boys in other noviciates being beaten or starved into submission. Smutty stories too, jokes about what some Brothers got up to; things he found hard to believe. So far he'd been lucky. Only one incident stood out. It had occurred during his second year, after he'd been given some flower-beds to look after. The beds had been neglected but with months of patient work he'd managed to put a shape on them, had grown to love his little patch of land. Even now, it was painful to remember the bewilderment, the horror he'd experienced arriving one morning to find his painstaking labour destroyed: shrubs and flowers torn up, rubbish dumped in their place. Fighting back tears, he'd gone to Ambrose, blurted out what had happened. Ambrose had listened, then in a voice bereft of emotion, explained it had been done deliberately. Pride, he'd informed Gerry, who hadn't yet taken his religious name, pride was a terrible sin and Gerry had been guilty of pride. The flower-beds didn't belong to him, nothing belonged to him, everything was done for the Glory of God. A novice's duty was to accept whatever came his way. With a wave of the hand, the older man had dismissed the boy, ordered him to start over again. Returning to the garden, Gerry had thrown himself on the ground. For a long time, he'd lain there, consumed with rage, until slowly, a kind of peace had descended; then he'd picked himself up, begun removing the debris in a quiet, orderly fashion. From a great distance, he'd watched himself, his anger dissipated.

Stanislaus filled a wheelbarrow with seed potatoes. His hands were raw from digging, and he wondered if maybe it wasn't too cold for sowing. Paddy's Day was still a couple of weeks off. At home it was the custom to have them sown before then; him and Josie did it, it was their job. What was she up to now, he wondered. A few months earlier, she'd taken a job in London, had been given special permission to visit before she left. He could still see her, holding a cigarette between scarlet nails, blowing smoke rings. What was it she'd said? "You're a free agent, Gerry. You can walk out those gates anytime." The gates she'd been referring to were visible from where Stanislaus was standing. The young man drew his eyes away, went back to the prepared drills, the waiting wheelbarrow. The spade slipped from his hand. The next moment he was walking. Within minutes, he'd reached the bottom of the avenue. If he intended going any distance, he should get a coat, a scarf, the wind was bitter; more snow had been forecast. Instead, he kept going, welcoming the pinch of weather as it nipped his neck, his face. Outside the grounds, he quickened his step, his breath white. For a while, his direction appeared aimless until he realised he was keeping parallel with the ridge of snow-capped mountains. Cars hurtled past. A bus lumbered into view. Recognising the destination, Stanislaus hailed it on impulse, the doors shutting before he realised he'd no money. Embarrassed, he pretended to search his pockets.

'Up to the old tricks, eh Father?' the driver joked.

Stanislaus was about to explain the man's mistake, people often mistook his collar for that of a priest but the driver waved him on. 'You're all right Father. Say a prayer for us.'

By the time the bus arrived at the terminus, Stanislaus was the only passenger. Pulling up the collar of his jacket, he stepped into the chill, leaving the muggy warmth behind. Unsure where he was going, he trudged along, past houses tucked behind windbreaks, mostly new-build, the sites ripped out of open countryside. The mountains were nowhere to be seen. Gauging their direction, he turned down a narrow boreen, tunnelled through stumps of pollarded trees, overgrown briar. The ground was shiny, rock hard and his new leather soles kept slipping. Now and again, he caught a glimpse of Dublin below him, a maze of buildings, like the Lego set Joe got for Christmas one year. As the lane petered into waste ground, a biting wind cut through his threadbare suit, stinging his legs and thighs. The mountains remained hidden but he slogged on, breath rasping. After what seemed ages, he reached the foothills, sprinkled with snow like icing sugar on a dark cake. Here the ground was fissured with half-thawed puddles, the fractured ice starred. His heart melted at the simple beauty of it and he pushed on, wind lashing his face, ears, making sails of his pants. He was almost at the snow line, outcrops lying in drifts, white and cold. He scooped a handful, put it to his tongue. It tasted of stale water. He scrambled on, wanting to be clear of the patches of dark earth, a burning sensation at the back of his throat, his feet sodden, one sock already disappeared into a shoe. He wondered where he was, if the place had a name? This bothered him, not knowing, then he forgot about it as his foot went from under him and he found himself tumbling. He landed on a bank, his left leg at an angle, snow burning his cheek. He heard himself laugh, an eerie sound, more like a whimper. When it died away, he tried to rise, found he couldn't. Dampness seeped through his clothes. Propping himself up, he saw, a little way off, a natural dip. Gritting his teeth, he inched forward, rolling the last few feet, pain searing his leg, travelling up through his body. The spot he landed in was out of the wind, protected. He lay there cradled in whiteness. The pain eased, slightly. Closing his eyes, he tried to pray but the words wouldn't come. He stared up at the sky, his mind blank. Time passed, minutes, hours. Overhead, the clouds took on shapes, reminding him of things, images mixing and melting into one another: his mother making bread, arms and dress dusted with flour, his father milking cows, Joe putting on his best white Sunday shirt, Josie in her Communion dress. He saw her spinning round, dress whirling. Then he saw himself as a child, five or six, lying in bed, his sister beside him, warm, comforting. It was getting near Christmas and they'd been hoping for snow.

'Will ye play?' Josie whispered. 'Ye promised.'

Nodding sleepily, he moved to the cold side of the bed, his sister to the far edge, her body hanging half out. From there she called in a faint voice as if she was a long way away. Gerry made a noise he hoped sounded like reindeers, then in a husky voice urged the animals on.

'Ye don't say 'gee-up' to reindeers,' Josie protested.

'How do you know?' he answered. 'Anyway, I'm coming, so get ready.'

Steering the sleigh this way and that, he skirted stars, clouds, glacial mountains topped with snow.

Josie called out again, louder.

'Who's that down there?' he shouted, grinding to a halt. 'Looks like a little girl to me.'

'Help,' Josie piped. 'I'm lost, I'm lost.'

Sprawling himself across the bed, he tried to yank her into the sleigh, Josie pretending to fall out, over and over, until she finally allowed herself be saved.

'Who are you?' she asked, wide-eyed.

'Don't you know, little girl?'

His sister shook her head.

'I'm Santa Claus, come to rescue you. On a snowy night like this you could freeze to death.'

Gerry opened his eyes, saw it was getting dark. In the distance Dublin glittered. Was that the end of the game? He couldn't remember. Maybe there was more or maybe they just fell asleep, cosy in each other's arms. He felt sleepy now, sleepy and surprisingly warm. Not frightened at all. In the waning light, the snow got brighter and brighter.

Cool And All Those Other Words

We're driving to the seaside and I'm congratulating myself on getting us out of the house without a screaming match or one of us in tears; I've even remembered Stella's sun-hat. Tamsin, my eldest, is sprawled across the back seat, defiance etched into the curl of her lips. If she catches my eye in the rear mirror, she'll accuse me of spying. Since she turned fifteen a couple of months ago, I've metamorphosed into a monster. Stella, who is three years younger, sits in front, clutching a new fluorescent holdall. The traffic stalls. Gauging by the number of vehicles, it looks as though half the country had the same bright idea.

'Mom,' (Tamsin adopted an American accent on her last birthday) 'Mom, it says here this sun cream lasts two hours. We'll have to put it on again when we arrive.'

'That's just to make people use more.'

'Why do you always say things like that!'

'Like what Tamsin? I'm trying to drive.'

'*Trying*,' she repeats under her breath.

I bite my tongue, begin counting to ten. A sports car, sunroof open, music blaring, shoots past on the hard shoulder.

'Christ!'

'Don't swear, Mammy,' Stella admonishes.

Tamsin stares longingly after the car. 'Cool,' she says.

Cool, I repeat to myself, that was one of our words.

'We'll rent a farm, grow our own food, keep hens. Think about it. It'll be so cool.' I can still remember Tom's enthusiasm as he talked me into giving up my second-floor flat to move to the back of nowhere. Something in my gut warned me but I was nineteen and in love; besides, I had no other plans. The farm turned out to be a derelict Land Commission cottage at the end of a dirt track. To say it was damp would be an understatement. The walls wept.

'You're a modern couple so,' our new landlord commented, a leery expression coming into his eyes as he handed Tom the key. His wife stared sourly at my ring-less finger, glared at her husband and stomped out. In bed that night, cuddled against the cold, we laughed it off, revelling in our coolness.

'Don't let Stella go in too deep,' I warn Tamsin as the two of them make for the blue stripe of water on the horizon. 'I'll be down later.' The shoreline's dotted with gyrating matchsticks, dashing in and out of the breakers, their squeals and the clamour of seagulls creating a kind of crazy excitement. I spread a sleeping bag and a couple of blankets beneath some overhanging rock, smile ruefully as a girl in a high-leg swimsuit sashays past, thinking how young she is despite a veneer of sophistication. Probably the same age I was when I set up home.

Love and youth got us through the first winter. I grew accustomed to the weeping walls just as I learned to accept the brown turfy water full of nameless bits which trickled down the mountain into a rusty tank on the shed roof. Other things took more getting used to: the hours digging and weeding the vegetable garden, my bones aching, hands in shreds; worst of all, my eyes red and sore from some kind of allergy. Tom didn't have to adapt. He was in his element. With puffy eyes, I'd watch him pore over seed catalogues, building journals, the dozens of do-it-yourself manuals which arrived by post, or listen as he talked earnestly to local farmers about what to grow where and when and how. Within weeks we had a cold frame and a compost heap. While Tom seemed to have found his life, I was losing mine. To survive the long, dark evenings, I taught myself to knit, sensing my soul slip away with each dropped stitch. Tom had a vision: buying a farm, becoming self-sufficient, growing organic crops; he talked about it endlessly. For a while I lived off his energy, afraid of admitting the truth, afraid of what it might do to our relationship. Dutifully, I nursed my hands, doctored my watering eyes, and like a sleeping princess, waited for someone or something to rescue me.

'Mammy, Mammy,' Stella calls from halfway up the beach, 'come and watch. Please!' I feel a rush of resentment. My body aches to lie undisturbed, to soak up the sun until I melt. On every spare inch of sand, adults and children goof about, playing rounders, cricket - squabbling and fighting good-humouredly. Envying their ease, I reach for my wrap. As I do, a ball skids past, sprays sand into my face.

'Sorry,' the culprit grins and I smile back, hiding my annoyance, hating myself for being so uptight.

Uptight. That's what Tom would throw at me whenever we had rows. 'Why can't you just enjoy what you're doing! You're so uptight.'

It's the kind of word that hits right below the belt. Knowing it was Tom's stock response to anyone who didn't see the world his way didn't lessen the sting. Why couldn't I enjoy what I was doing? What was wrong with me? Then two things happened. I got pregnant and I realised I didn't love Tom.

I didn't tell him, I could hardly bear admitting it to myself. But I could use the baby. For its sake, I argued, we could not go on living in a damp freezing house, never sure where the next penny was coming from. We'd have to move to a town, get jobs, it wasn't just the two of us any longer. Secretly I hoped my demands would provoke a split but Tom offered a compromise: he'd find us a new place, somewhere with proper heating, get a part-time job so we'd have a regular income. Scared of being alone, I capitulated. As with everything, Tom set his mind to the task and within a month he'd got himself a bread delivery round and we were ensconced in a small comfortable cottage near a beach with a couple of acres for growing stuff.

The beach saved me. I grew to love it, walking its length several times daily, getting to know each rock and rock-pool, every fresh bit of driftwood, the myriad shells it harboured, the seaweed slapping and sucking at the shoreline. Inside me, the baby grew in its own pool, moved in its own mysterious waters. As time passed, I wished for it to grow as strong as the sea battering the sea-wall at night and as calm and peaceful as the foam caressing my toes at the beginning of that long stormy period that changed everything.

Tamsin got strength all right. From the water's edge, I watch her swim like a mermaid, then disappear for what seems like an eternity. My heart races until she re-appears, scales of water dropping like golden coins.

'Wow! You can really swim.'

'I can swim too,' Stella pouts, kicking her legs and splashing me.

Noticing my discomfort, Tamsin scoops a handful of water.

'Don't!' I scream. Despite my love of the sea, I've never learned to swim, hate getting wet.

A look of scorn flits across Tamsin's face as she allows the water leak from her hands. Diving in, she swims to where Stella is laboriously practising doggy paddles. I want to re-wind the clock, take back my words, let her throw the water, be the kind of mother I know she wants me to be: fun, spontaneous, easy. I love Tamsin, I love both my kids but bringing them up alone I had never enough energy or time to enjoy them. I was too young when Tamsin was born, too angry and lonely by the time Stella arrived.

The fights became more frequent, the intervals between them shorter. Most centred around me feeling dumped on with all the childcare and housework. As it happened the one that finally blew it was over a convoy of New Agers who'd set up camp on a piece of land between our property and the shore.

'Who do they think they are!' Tom yelled, stomping round the kitchen, 'trespassing on other people's land.'

'Trespassing! They could be us, a few years ago.'

'We rented a house, paid for it. I'm going down to clear them off!' He made for the door.

'Don't. I'll talk to them, persuade them to leave.' Pushing past him, I grabbed Tamsin from under the table where she'd gone to hide.

A huge fire glowed eerily in the centre of the encampment, sending out a hazy heat that blurred the air, making everyday things seem unreal. Too shy to call out, I hovered, waiting for someone to notice me. The women squatting by the coals looked content, capable, the men indolent, some with their eyes closed, some smoking, one flat on his back, strumming a guitar. A handful of half-naked kids, baked brown by sun, played in the dirt. On the few scraggy bushes bordering the camp, brightly coloured clothes had been spread to dry, adding another layer of make-believe.

Tamsin stared bug-eyed, fascinated by the fire, the kids, the rainbow clothes. Watching her watching them, I felt the pull of a carefree existence, an ache to let go of responsibility, schedules, back breaking work.

A thin guy who'd been sitting at the back of a painted van ambled over and offered me a toke. I shook my head apologetically. 'No sweat. You live around here?' He had an English accent, eyes like dark mirrors.

'In the cottage, over there,' I pointed.

'Far out. Mystical.' He smiled, a big kiddish smile that reached all the way to my heart. 'I'm Fern.'

'I'm Roisin and this is ... Tamsin.'

'Far out,' he repeated. 'Wish I was Irish, it's so beautiful here. People are beautiful too.'

I blushed.

'Come and meet the others,' he invited, holding out a hand to Tamsin, 'they won't bite. Course, Fern's not my real name.'

'What is it?'

'Promise not to laugh? It's Sidney. After Sidney James, the comedian. My Dad thought he was the greatest.'

Fern made the introductions. Everyone was so laid back, friendly, especially the women, who seemed to float, conjuring up cups of herbal tea, offering to plait Tamsin's hair, paint her face. One woman, wearing a long purple gown with a hood, handed me a feather. It was white and as I smiled my thanks I wondered if she'd guessed why I was there. Feeling a complete hypocrite, I sat staring into the coals, inwardly cursing Tom until the guy with the guitar suddenly asked if I knew the best route to Donegal and it became obvious they were leaving in a couple of days.

'Wanna play horsies?' Fern asked, reaching for Tamsin, his eyes locking with mine. As they clip-clopped round the trailers, Tamsin shrieking and giggling, the relief I'd been feeling at not having to say anything turned into something else. Moments later, when Fern opened his van to give Tamsin a peek, I craned my neck, surreptitiously checking for signs of a woman's presence.

'Come down later,' he suggested as I waved goodbye, 'we're having a sing-song, smoke if you're into it.' His hand caught mine.

'I'll see,' I answered, the imprint of his fingers burning.

I didn't go but when Tom left for his bread round next morning, I bundled up a sleeping Tamsin, walked quickly down the boreen. As soon as I saw Fern, we both knew. Slipping out of his jacket, he draped it round my shoulders, led me to his van. With the baby sleeping peacefully beside us we made love.

'Life could be so simple,' he murmured, stroking my hair. 'All we have to do is get rid of property, institutions, throw away all the rule books.'

I nodded, wanting to believe him; another part of me was listening for the sound of Tom's car. 'Why don't you come with us? Bring Tamsin. Can't go without baby.'

'But ...'

'It would be so cool.'

Tamsin stirred and Fern picked her up, plonked her on his chest. 'This is a free spirit, man. She doesn't want to be buried under a whole heap of rules and regulations.' He ran a finger along my arm. 'Your choice, dig? We're splitting early, about six.' He grinned at Tamsin who dimpled. 'Hey, you talk some sense to this chick, put in a good word for me huh?'

After a picnic lunch, I give Tamsin money to get her and Stella ice-creams. They're back in a short while, licking and sucking, dragging a tall kid with them. Tamsin tells me her name is Jane; asks if they can hang out with her and her friends on the far side of the beach. The girl points, waves, and a couple of indistinct figures wave back.

'Okay, I can see you from here. But nowhere else. And Tamsin, keep an eye on Stella.'

They hurry away, laughing and skitting, Tamsin's bright pink swimsuit and Stella's electric blue visible as they recede. I bask in my freedom for a little while before a feeling of loneliness takes over. My thoughts drift to Tom and I wonder what he's up to. After we finally broke up, he went to Canada to study methods of seed harvesting. I stopped hearing from him soon after Stella was born. Later, through a mutual friend I learned he'd changed his mind about marriage, had hitched up with some Canadian. I think of the seed he planted in me.

I wake with a start, glance instantly over to where the girls should be but can't see either of them. Panic rising, I scan the countless bodies thronging the beach, swivel my gaze towards the horizon. They've probably gone for a swim, I assure myself, racing down the strand. As I reach the water, a figure straightens. It's Tamsin. She and Jane are tossing water over one another, managing to splash a couple of gangly boys who are pretending not to notice.

'Where's Stella!' I scream above the roar of waves.

Tamsin doesn't hear. When she finally notices me, she's embarrassed, rushes over as if to shield me from the others. 'I'm not doing anything,' she hisses.

'Where's Stella?'

Her eyes swing towards the rocks.

'I was only in the water a few minutes,' she defends herself.

We hurry to where several towels are spread out.

'She was here a minute ago - they all were- '

'She didn't go into the water after you?'

'No, no!'

I narrow my eyes, scour the periphery of the beach. 'You know Stella can't swim. You know that, don't you!'

Jane joins us, stands with her mouth open. 'Where are the others?' Tamsin demands, sounding like me.

Jane shrugs, climbs up on a small rise, eyes squinting. 'There they are - over there!' She points towards a circle of girls digging in the sand. I follow her finger, see no sign of a blue swimsuit.

'Have you seen Stella?' I call from a few feet away, trying to mask the terror in my voice. A girl with a ponytail grins mischievously at me; the rest carry on shovelling.

I'm about to lose it when I hear Stella's voice. 'I'm here Mammy, look. They're burying me.'

I sink to the ground beside her, kiss her, mussing the sand, getting it all over me. 'Oh Stella, I was so worried. I thought you'd gone off ... into the water.'

'But you always tell me not to. That's the rule.'

I hold her tight, feel Tamsin slide down, wind her arms round both of us. She's shivering. 'I love us all,' I say hugging them to me.

'You've ruined it now,' Stella complains.

'Would you like me to bury you again?'

'Will you Mammy? Really?'

I nod, smile, feel something shift inside me.

It was still dark when I woke Tamsin, warning her to be quiet so as not to waken Daddy. The early morning silence carried faint sounds of doors clanging, engines coughing and I pictured myself getting into one of the snug green vans, Fern at the wheel. Buttoning Tamsin's coat, I could hear his cajoling voice; felt again the lure of a life without ties, travelling where and when we wanted to. My daughter gurgled and I picked her up. As I carried her to the window, she looked at me, eyes big and trusting. The rumble of engines got louder; a van stopped by the gate.

'Mama,' Tamsin pointed.

I stepped back but not quick enough to avoid seeing Fern stick his head out a window. Part of me wanted to run out to him while another part knew this dream of a free and easy life was his dream, just as the cottage in the country with the home-grown vegetables had been Tom's. I held onto Tamsin, took a deep breath. The convoy moved on.

To the east the sky reddened and a large golden ball began its slow ascent. 'We're going to watch the sun rising,' I murmured in a soothing voice, needing something to cling to. 'It rises every morning, sets each evening.'

A month later I left Tom.

On the way home from the beach, we sing songs, one after the other, making up the words when we can't remember them. 'I really enjoyed today, Mammy,' Tamsin says, as we pull into the driveway in front of the house. 'It was fun,' Stella adds. 'Can we go again next week?' She snuggles in, makes pleading eyes. 'Please?'

'Cool,' I say and we all laugh.

Biddy's Research

Biddy never took any chances. She knew there was a world-wide conspiracy. That men were in the firing line sometimes proved nothing. Besides, in those circumstances it was often referred to as happening to "people". And things were not divided evenly either, not by a long shot. Outside of wars and Acts of God, it was women who were being killed, murdered, exterminated - call it any name you like - the result was the same. She might not have all the statistics but who believed statistics anyway?

So Biddy took precautions.

She avoided crossing streets near banks, even at pedestrian crossings, if a security van or what looked like a getaway car was parked in the vicinity. That was courting disaster as one woman had discovered only recently. My God, she'd never realised how many banks there were in Dublin. Banks themselves were no-go areas. She corresponded with one but that was as far as it went. She refused to have gas in her home - five explosions - this year alone! Electricity was so much cleaner even if it was more expensive. It's an ill-wind, she thought, whenever prices shot up. Cycling, swimming and jogging were all out but Biddy kept as fit as anybody, running on the spot in the comfort of her own home. All of which had the added advantage of giving her more time to concentrate on her Research.

Sitting back from her columns, Biddy chewed a pencil. She had films to thank for opening her eyes. Biddy loved the cinema. There was nothing she loved better than sitting in the dark, munching popcorn, following the progress of one or other of her favourite female stars. Over time, though, it began to dawn on her that with the exception of musicals, the chances of a woman surviving the entire length of a film were low, leading lady or not. Psycho clinched it. To be completely fair (and Biddy felt this was essential to her work) the odd one survived if death by boredom didn't count. Having never been troubled by the question whether art mirrored life or life art (or indeed if cinema was art), Biddy allowed these observations hover round her subconscious until one day sitting in her comfy chair she realised it wasn't only in films women were being killed! It was happening in real life: and to the bit parts as well as the heroines! Shortly afterwards, Biddy had tried her discovery out on a friend. 'I think,' she'd begun (she was not the sort of person to force her opinions on others) 'I think women are being bumped off...?' To her surprise, the woman had agreed profusely, only to drag the dreaded word "people" into the conversation within minutes. Biddy sighed, did nobody notice, care? Returning to her work, she re-read the previous page (she'd reached the stage of differentiating between the 'accidental', those that happened to people, and the 'planned', those that happened to women) shaking her head. Surely, if it were a fact of life, her mother would have warned her. Unless she thought Biddy might worry herself to death. Biddy smiled. It was true she was the worrying kind and so was her mother. Now she understood why, she wished she'd been more patient with her. Growing up, she'd simply gone along with her father when he said, "If your mother didn't have something to worry about, she'd make it up." Easy for him to talk, he wasn't an endangered species.

No sooner had Biddy put her fingers to the keyboard than she was on her feet. Up and down she paced, weaving in and around the endless piles of papers she'd accumulated. A headline caught her eye. 'DEAD AFTER SMILING IN PUB'. She stopped. It had to be acknowledged that those responsible for this conspiracy weren't utterly heartless. If you read the papers thoroughly and paid careful attention to the media, plenty of clues were given about what to avoid and how to make the most of your chances. Glancing at her watch, she saw it was time for the mid-day news. Turning on the radio, she allowed the broadcaster's silky voice lull her as she listened absently to reports about the Middle East, further recession in America. Then Biddy's practised ear discerned a slight change in the broadcaster's tone. Her heart quickened. Earlier that morning, he announced, in what appeared to be a tragic accident, a woman had been killed after touching some railings in a park. The railings - here he cleared his throat - had somehow become connected to a mains supply of electricity. Accident! Biddy snorted. Who did they think they were fooling? Glumly, she sat down. Where was this going to end? What would happen as she got older and her memory failed? Would she remember all the danger areas or would she spend the last years of her life trapped in her own home for fear of making a mistake? Mulling over her thoughts, Biddy went to the kitchen to make lunch. Turning on the grill, she found it hard not to have second thoughts about her electric cooker.

On her way to a newspaper library that afternoon Biddy ploughed through Dublin traffic, wondering again whether 'collisions' should be moved to the 'planned' category. Of course, driving had advantages; it meant never having to walk anywhere late at night, never having to take taxis and never, never having to hitch a lift - all potentially fatal situations. It also meant she could wear what she liked, so that a blouse or a skirt or the cut of her jeans could not put paid to what she loved so dearly. There was another reason for driving which Biddy didn't like admitting. The truth was her right eye had a slight nervous tick that in certain circumstances could be construed as a wink. A defect such as this, while not exactly lethal, certainly stacked the dice against her. To offset it, Biddy wore dark glasses and preferred going everywhere by car. She wasn't one to take chances especially now her Research was going so well. Biddy smiled into the rear mirror. 'I'm going to expose this conspiracy if it's the last thing I do,' she vowed.

After a hard afternoon's work Biddy returned to the car park. An empty space greeted her. Removing her glasses, she looked frantically about but her car was nowhere to be seen. Realising her eye was going a mile a minute, she put her glasses back on. Then, helpless with fury, Biddy hurried to the nearest police station, thanking her lucky stars it was summer and still bright at six o'clock.

In the weeks that followed Biddy wore a boiler suit and glasses wherever she went and made all her appointments during the day. Despite this, her work was being held up. Recently, she'd made contact with a woman named Grainne, a kindred spirit it would appear, who'd written or attempted to write a thesis on the subject. It was vital they meet. Unfortunately, the woman was now living in a Therapeutic Community and for some reason would see women only after dark. Biddy weighed up the pros and cons. Could she, in the interests of her work, do something she hadn't done for several years: risk travelling on public transport? Alone? At night?

Since her latest research suggested that looking like a person was an advantage, Biddy donned a pair of strong boots and tucked her hair into a beret before setting out on her adventure. Arriving safely, she had a long discussion with Grainne (who struck her as eminently sane) which revealed that the two of them had arrived at the same conclusion, albeit from different directions. Both were convinced neither people nor persons existed in any real sense, that there were in fact only men and women. However when Biddy confessed she'd reached an impasse at precisely this point, her new acquaintance nodded knowingly.

'It's probably staring us in the face,' Grainne moaned.

Sadly they said goodbye, promising to contact one another if either felt they'd cracked it. Walking down the long, winding, dark road to the nearest bus stop Biddy was so engrossed by the problem she almost forgot her danger. Then remembering that walking slowly could be misinterpreted - a court case had established that - she hurried along looking neither right nor left while at the same time remaining aware of every leaf on every tree and the slightest movement of even a sweet wrapper on the pavement. A woman tottering past on high heels flashed Biddy a grateful look. Oh my God, Biddy thought, has nobody warned her about foot-ware? She sighed. The sooner her Research was published the better.

Reaching the bus stop, Biddy noticed a person was already waiting. A man, she corrected herself. Her right eye began to twitch. Thank God for glasses, she thought. Moments later, she admitted to herself she was afraid. The man appeared to be watching her. In fact, she was sure he'd moved ever so slightly in her direction. Her mouth dried. Was this it? Was this one of the exterminators? What should she do? For a moment her mind went blank then the words of an old song her mother used to sing popped into her head ....

"Whenever I feel afraid I hold my head erect
And whistle a happy tune so no one will suspect
I'm afraid."

Holding her head as erect as possible Biddy whistled. A weird sound emanated from her lips. It was so weird it made her laugh out loud. The man looked at her, edged away. She whistled again, then, letting go of caution, banged on some iron railings to keep in tune. He probably thinks I'm mad, she thought. Maybe they're afraid of mad people, I mean, mad women. She laughed again as a bus trundled into view.

Biddy stared from the lighted bus. I've survived, she congratulated herself, then her heart did a little dance. The answer she was looking for was as plain as the darkness outside. How could she have missed it - the whole thing was too obvious for words! All the same, she concluded, after some reflection, it was the only possible explanation. Her Research was over. Relishing her discovery, Biddy sat back and for the first time in years smiled openly in a public place.

Just wait 'till I phone Grainne, she thought.

Portrait of the Artist

Graham woke with a familiar feeling of emptiness. In search of diversion, his eyes flitted around the bedroom, coming to rest on a small self-portrait, a chance find in a Parisian flea market. He studied the strong lines, the unflinching gaze. Strange he'd never attempted one himself. Could he be afraid of provoking fate like those indigenous people he'd read about who'd refused to have their photographs taken, believing cameras had the power to steal their souls? Not that this belief had saved them. More than one way to skin a cat, he shrugged, forcing himself out of bed. The cliché hung in the air as he struggled on with his dressing gown. On his way downstairs, he caught sight of his reflection in a mirror. His own soul? What had become of that?

Mozart at full volume, Graham stood washing breakfast dishes at the kitchen sink. In the normal run of things, he allowed them pile up, tackling them when he ran out or mould appeared. Now the chore filled a tiny part of the gaping hole called morning. He was having what is euphemistically called a 'dry spell', nothing to do with the weather. When it began it hadn't perturbed him unduly, he'd been expecting it to run a course similar to other fallow periods: creeping boredom, anger, a letting go; then a return to work feeling renewed, invigorated. *A weathering of the soul.* He'd come across the phrase somewhere, describing a state of loneliness, a kind of despair artists experience, willingly take on sometimes for the sake of their art. But as the weeks turned to months, Graham sensed this wasn't like other times. Nine months had gone by. The gestation period for a baby. Had Lona wanted a child? She'd never said she did, not in so many words. Of course, he'd been fairly frank about his desire for freedom - from certain kinds of responsibility: freedom to work. The irony wasn't lost on him. Or on James, his agent, already voicing frustration at his lack of output. Why wouldn't he, as the locals liked to put it: Graham was a lucrative client, his last exhibition had sold outright the first night. "Rich and dense as geological layers", one critic had extolled. "You're on a roll, punters can't get enough of you." James' words.

Picking up a glass, Graham polished it until his face gleamed back at him: distorted, gargoylesque. What was it some woman had written: you could neither be too rich nor too thin. How about too successful? Certainly, after years of waiting, it had been exhilarating to see his landscapes become flavour of the month. Then flavour of the year. A successful show in California and he'd been on the pig's back. Another cliché. What did it mean? A pig's back was hardly a comfortable place, not one you could ride on for long. Should an artist be there at all? Opening a cabinet, Graham replaced the glass. What had art to do with comfort anyway? Weren't artists in the business of making others uncomfortable? People queuing to buy his work could be interpreted as a sign of failure. But what kind, that was the question. Artistic? Or a failure of integrity? Both?

Having spread the soggy tea towel along a radiator, Graham took up a position at the bay window. He did this most days, noting the imperceptible changes heralding spring: burgeoning knots on the ashes, catkins lengthening, a light dusting of green on his one arable field. Only the belt of ground he thought of as the *wasteland*, a dense thicket of thorn and scrub bordering his farm, retained its wintry pallor. It was this feature which had attracted him most when he'd come to view the place; it amused him to think of living in a house surrounded by almost impenetrable brush, a sanctuary for foxes, badgers, feral goats, animals known to keep their distance. This morning nothing stirred, other than a bank of bulbous grey clouds puffing across the horizon. He'd be puffing his way to the pub soon. Graham patted his midriff. He'd grown stout at Briar Cottage, a wall of flesh between him - and what? His gaze homed in on a purpose-built studio, its newness partially disguised by a plaiting of clematis. Sunk in shadow, it had a forlorn aspect. As he watched, part of the shadow detached itself and a cat emerged, paws barely touching the ground. Graham's eyebrows shot up. Was it Jet? Could she have found her way back after all this time?

Hunkering and making meow sounds, Graham scoured the area where he'd seen the animal. Clumps of primroses, their buttery lights waning, eyed him sadly. Jet - if it was her - had vanished. Just what he should do if he'd any sense. The painter heaved himself up. The truth was, he couldn't leave. Something held him, it was as if he was under a spell, a *geis*. He glanced towards the studio, began walking in its direction. Might as well get the morning ritual over, he thought, unlatching the door. The studio was large, with a long narrow table running the full length. Light from a glass roof lit it beautifully. Graham stood in the light, face to face with a large empty canvas. Shifting weight from one foot to the other, he screwed up his eyes, then reaching for a tube of paint squirted a blob onto a square of plastic. Carefully, he chose a brush from one of the jam jars crammed with them. His eyes moved thoughtfully from brush to paint, paint to canvas. Five minutes passed. The sound of his breathing filled the silence. Ten minutes. With an impatient gesture, he turned and walked quickly from the room.

Ensconced in his retreat beneath the pub window, Graham sipped a whisky, wondering, not for the first time, whether his move to the country had been a mistake. Success, he had discovered, had a downside: too many phone calls, unwelcome invitations, worst of all, people expecting things from him. When his work began to suffer Briar Cottage had appeared like an answer to prayer. There, only the invited came. The locals, intrigued someone would choose to live in such a godforsaken place, had accepted him immediately, then left him alone for the most part. Of course, there were times he felt lonely, especially when his relationship with Lona ended. Was it coincidence she and the cat chose the same week-

'There y'are Mr Graham!' The reddened face of Seamus Mooney towered over the table, his body swaying to find the perpendicular. Seamus, a bachelor with a pack of greyhounds that yelped furiously whenever Graham passed, made a point of button-holing him whenever he had a bit too much to drink. 'Ye know, I was thinking I might tek up this art lark mesel. Shure childer could paint as good, am I right?' He turned and winked at the occupants of the bar.

Graham saluted, reached for his paper.

'Tell me Mr Graham, d'ye never get fed up painting that auld landscape? Maybe want to paint something different?'

'What about you?' Graham countered, 'cutting turf every year. Ever get tired of that?'

'I do indeed and curse it, shure doing anythin' over and over would drive a body mad.'

'Anything?'

'Anythin'.' Seamus looked slyly round, begging approval.

'What about drinking?'

'Snookered ye,' someone jeered. A couple of others laughed obligingly.

Seamus' mouth twisted in a roguish smile. 'Faith, ye have me there.' His head shook in disbelief. Lifting a pint to his mouth, he finished it in one go, shouted for another. As he waited for the stout to settle, he launched into a rambling story. Graham half-listened, preoccupied with the man's original question. Maybe he had grown tired of repeating himself, painting the same thing again and again, becoming more and more famous in the process. Wasn't that what Duchamps had railed against? Perhaps he should follow in the dead artist's footsteps: abandon painting, turn what was happening into a crusade. There was no shortage of things to protest about: art reduced to product, painters as personalities.

'Be seeing you,' he said. Time to hit the road when he found himself thinking like that.

'I was just getting to the good bit,' Seamus protested.

Fumbling for house keys, he saw her. Back arched, fur distended, each hair an antenna, the cat skulked along the wall, her tail forming a question mark. It was definitely Jet, her prowl was unmistakable. Graham watched as she sidled knowingly towards the door of the studio, stopping along the way to rub an ear against concrete. The cat flap! Why hadn't he thought of it? For months after she disappeared, he'd left it open, finally nailing it up when a mangy stray tried to take up residence. Exasperated, Graham exhaled. Instantly, the animal was mid-air, her elongated body hurtling towards the wasteland. In one swift movement, she scaled an outcrop of rocks at the edge of the brush, spinning round at the summit, a challenge in the look she flashed him. Breathing heavily, Graham clambered after her, stones giving way beneath his boots. His eyes scanned the terrain for a hint of black but she'd gone to ground, vanished like the goats he'd disturbed one morning, their horns like demented handlebars, a smell so rank it choked. Had Jet thrown her lot in with a herd of wild goats? The thought she might have chosen their company over his unsettled him.

The following day, Graham laid saucers of milk and dishes of food around the house then pulling a chair to the kitchen window, set up watch. When Jet hadn't appeared by midday, he decided to forego his usual trip to the pub. Over a glass of wine, he idled over possible scenarios that might solve the predicament he'd found himself in: in one he sold up and went back to the city, tail between his legs; in another he locked himself into the studio, forced himself to work. He even considered the merits of getting so atrociously drunk he might do anything. Something. The afternoon dragged on, his thoughts taking a different tack as he ransacked his past for a clue, an explanation. No one thing suggested itself, no moment or decision. The move might have precipitated it or the break-up of his relationship, success might have played a part. His life, as far as he could make out, was composed of a series of events he'd participated in, engineered even, but how one led to the next seemed shrouded in mystery. At any point, he might have made different choices, taken a different route, become a different person. Was he the person he was meant to be? Who could tell? He dozed off at some stage, woke to find it had grown dark. Deflated, he decided to give up his vigil. Cutting a chunk of cheddar, he thought of Jet roaming free in her tangled world, envied her. He took the remains of the wine upstairs but when he eventually settled down, sleep eluded him, his mind treading the same ground: what had brought him to this impasse? Who was he if he didn't paint? Then, from nowhere, an idea began to form ...

Graham arranged nine canvasses - one large, four pairs with similar dimensions - into a semicircle, the largest at the centre. He'd spent a week stretching, priming; now they were ready. He drained his early morning mug of coffee, savouring the pungent liquid, the finished paintings vivid in his mind. As he imagined them, each would be complete in its own terms - but - and this would be the challenge, viewed together they'd form a whole. At first the idea of using photographs had appealed to him but in the end he'd decided to rely on memory although it had been years since he'd done anything figurative, never mind something of this magnitude. His pulse quickened. Picking up a brush, he dipped it into the wash.

The morning passed quickly. He ate a makeshift lunch waiting for the canvases to dry, eager to get back to them. The afternoon was taken up with sketching outlines, working shapes, moving from composition to composition, trying to find the point at which one slipped naturally into the other. He worked quickly, translating thought to medium, throwing himself into it. As soon as he was satisfied, he placed tubs of paint at different locations round the studio so that nothing could impede his flow. Night fell. He continued. On his way back to the house, he noticed that some of the food he'd left out had been eaten although there was no way of telling what had eaten it.

During the days that followed, Graham worked flat out, returning dog-tired each evening. Towards the end of the first feverish week, he realised he'd been going about it all wrong, was forced to ditch everything, start over. The second time round, he allowed the paint dictate, knowing it was possible, knowing all he had to do was trust.

Away from the studio, he made sketches, tried various arrangements in miniature to see the effect, cursed, prayed, felt truly alive for the first time in years. To guard against intrusion, he took the phone off the hook, gave up going to the pub. At some point he stopped shaving. Eventually, he stopped noticing. Only the work mattered. The work was everything. Now he had to sit with it, let it find its own pace, be content with playing second fiddle. He resumed his old habit of smoking, circling the paintings for hours, willing their completion, restless for it to be over.

At last the day arrived and Graham went from canvas to canvas putting in the final touches. When he was satisfied, he closed the studio door, made his way to the field bordering the wasteland. He was shocked to find it overgrown, ragwort and umbelliflor running wild, some as high as his shoulders. Taking out a pack of cigarettes, he lit one, smoked it. Ritual completed, he threw away the pack. Walking back to the house, he passed rows of dirty dishes, pocked with morsels of dried food, realised he hadn't thought about Jet in ages. Indoors, he rang James, whistled softly while his agent subjected him to a tirade of abuse. When he'd had enough, Graham told him to go to hell, refusing to explain what he'd been up to, inviting him to come and see for himself. Eventually James relented, promising to round up a few people, make a night of it. That sorted, he phoned Lona. Getting no response, he left a message on her voice-mail.

After a soak, shave and a much-needed change of clothes, Graham gave into an impulse to have one last look before people began arriving. It was almost dusk and the ash trees bordering the path to the studio were poised like paper cut-outs against the pearly sky. Light and dark. *Chiaroscuro.* A sudden feeling of being indistinguishable from his surroundings filled Graham. He stopped. Instantly, he intuited the cat's presence. Holding his breath, he watched Jet emerge from beneath a bush, pad past, paws dropping slow motion, so close he felt a brush of fur against his leg. She was making for the wasteland. Spurred by the drone of her purr, he followed, certain she was aware of him.

Clothes snagged, hands scratched and bloody, Graham admitted defeat. Once again Jet had eluded him and with darkness falling, he was lost into the bargain. Squinting at the luminous dial on his watch, he calculated that James and whoever he'd mustered would be arriving soon. If they made enough noise, he might be able to find his bearings. Bent double, hands outstretched to protect his face, he moved cautiously, searching for an opening. Nuts crunched beneath his feet, brushwood cracked. Every way he turned, hazel and blackthorn impeded his path. What, he wondered, had brought about such an unlikely coupling: one the tree of knowledge, the other considered unlucky, its vicious thorns a barrier to intrusion. Meditating on their improbable marriage, laughter erupted deep inside Graham; he laughed and laughed, tears streaming down his face. A wave of exhaustion followed. He slumped, found the dry, mossy earth waiting. The thicket grew clamorous, invisible birds twittering, shrilling. Sometime later, he wasn't certain how long, sounds that might have been a car, or several cars, were audible above the chorus. Moons of light appeared in the distance. He thought of shouting. The noises died away, the lights went out. All that was left was birdcall. Graham's eyes closed, lulled by the repetition. Dreamily, he conjured up the paintings, tried to predict James' reaction. Delight? Disbelief? What of the others? Disappointment at this departure from his usual preoccupations? And Lona? Would she be the first to grasp that viewed together the canvasses made a portrait? Portrait of the artist. The hazel and the blackthorn: Graham laughed, less heartily this time. Some way off, a cat meowed. So Jet hadn't led him a merry dance after all. In the morning he'd leave Briar Cottage. No need for him to be here now. No need at all.

Away Games

Olive parks badly, swears. Her son is visible through the school railings, sitting on a low wall, legs dangling.

'Colm!' she yells.

He glances in her direction, goes back to studying the ground. Something's wrong, she senses it. As she approaches he keeps his face averted; when she draws level he turns it to her almost defiantly. Olive gasps. 'Jesus!' She folds him in her arms, pulls back to inspect his swollen nose and mouth, the blood caked above his lip.

'What happened? Were ye in a fight? Ye know ye shouldn't be fighting.'

Colm doesn't answer. Instead, he begins to swing his legs vigorously, studying the movement as if his life depended on it, blocking her out in the process.

'Will ye not tell your mammy what ye were fighting about?' she coaxes, stroking him gently.

Removing his arm from her touch, Colm props up his chin, stares into the distance.

Olive gives up. 'It's all right. Sure, you can tell me when we get home. There's a good boy.'

But Colm won't budge and the grim look on his face while she washes off the dried blood frightens Olive. After she's smeared on a bit of antiseptic, he sits at the table, silent, morose. She sighs, switches on the microwave, her mind idling over the evening ahead: Friday, she and Steve can relax, open a bottle ... A headline in the Evening Standard catches her eye: ENGLAND MUST WIN! Fuck, she forgot the bloody World Cup was on. Steve would want to watch it. Hope they lose, she mutters to herself, clearing breakfast dishes into the sink. Surreptitiously, she glances at her son, still hunched in the same position, wonders what's going on in his head. The microwave beeps.

'Your favourite,' she cajoles, setting down fish fingers and chips; is rewarded with a half-hearted smile. 'C'mon, you can tell Mammy.' She runs a hand through the boy's soft hair. Colm ignores her, playing with the food, his eyes stuck to the plate. When he eventually raises them, they have a challenging look she's never seen before.

'Mammy, am I Irish?'

Olive has been expecting so many horrors she almost laughs with relief.

'Of course you're Irish. Haven't we been home loads of times to where Granny and all your cousins ...' A thought strikes her. 'Has someone been saying you're not?' She feels her temper rise. The school he goes to has a fair sprinkling of second and third generation Irish, these days even first generation. She chose it for that reason, wanting him to have contact with other Irish kids, families – a sort of bulwark against the avalanche of English culture. Or lack of it, as she might tease Steve. Was some bastard getting at her son because his father is English?

'Is that what you were fighting over? Poor baby ...'

She goes to hug him but he pushes her away.

'But I was born in England, wasn't I?'

'That doesn't matter. It's not important where you're born.' Olive stops. Even she doesn't believe that. How could she? Quickly, she sorts out her thoughts. 'I mean, it is important, but it's not the only important thing. I'm Irish, you're my child so you're Irish. You'd have been born in Ireland, if things, history and all that had been different.'

On firmer ground, she hurries on. 'It's like a feeling, you know you're Irish even if you're born here.' She pauses. Can an eight-year-old understand what she's getting at?

'But Daddy's English and I was born in England. That's two things, that makes me English.'

'That's what I'm trying to explain. It doesn't. Ye mustn't mind what kids say. You're Irish and you're proud of it.'

Colm shoves the plate away, jumps up from the table. At the door he turns, his face ashen.

'I'm not, I'm not. That's what they were saying and I fought them.' His eyes blaze.

'I'm English.'

'Thanks.' Olive takes the glass of wine, breaths it in briefly before downing half in one go. She settles back onto a pillow. 'God, I needed that.'

Steve pushes the duvet down, feels round for the remote control.

'Did ye know because people switch off with remotes instead of pulling out the plug, they use up enough electricity to power Leicester for a day. Or is it Liverpool?'

'Is that what you learned at school today? Well teacher-,' Steve breaks off, ups the volume. 'Wait, it's started. You sure you want to watch?'

'Have I any choice?'

'You could do the ironing.' He drapes an arm round her. 'Maybe seeing England getting thrashed will cheer you up.' He glances across to the screen. 'The kick-off isn't for another fifteen minutes. Want me to speak to Colm?'

'No. Leave him alone. He's reading. Ye know, Steve, I've been thinking. Remember I was going to have him in Ireland? Wish I had now. Suppose I thought it was, like I was trying to tell him, a gut feeling being Irish. It's probably a phase he's going through.'

'Thanks a bunch. Some of us are stuck with it.'

'Sorry' is on the tip of Olive's tongue when a thought occurs to her. She stares at the black curly hairs on the neck of the man she married nine years earlier, follows the contour of his hairline to the almost kiss curl that hangs over his eyes. She fell in love with that profile, with those eyes. Eyes now staring intently while a group of men, Englishmen like him, discuss the prospects of the English team. She listens to the various accents, identifies them without thinking, Cockney, West Country, a thick nasal Mancunian. She blurts out the thought.

'Ye know, I've never really thought of you as English. I know you are but ...'

'That's probably a compliment.' Her husband looks her straight in the face. 'Colm has a point. He's half and half, in fact a little more English if you weigh it up.'

Not quickly enough, Olive tries to banish a second thought: that she would never, could never, have married an Englishman. What did that mean? Christ! Whatever it means, she isn't going to think about it. Not right this moment. Anyway, it's Colm she's concerned with.

'That's not true. I brought him up Irish.'

'Just pulling your leg.'

'Well don't.'

Steve is silent for a moment. 'I envy you sometimes. You mightn't think it but it would be nice to feel proud of where you come from. I know, we've got Shakespeare and Bristol Rovers but-'

Olive punches him playfully.

'If you're feeling like this maybe you shouldn't watch, you might start attacking me.'

Olive needs to watch the match, needs a diversion from the thoughts spinning in her head. 'I want to see England trounced by Morocco. Bet they think they can waltz home.'

Steve squeezes her. 'Didn't know you were a secret football fan. Here, it's starting.'

'Hard not to be. Tim and Richard talk about nothing else in the staff-room. I could give a blow-by-blow account of how England lost to Portugal the other night. Sorry, how Portugal 'stole' the match. England, as you know, never lose -'

'Hope you're not going to talk all the way through it,' Steve interrupts.

'Fuck off.' Olive shuts up, forcing herself to focus on the two groups of men in different coloured shirts battling for the ball. She makes an effort to join her mind to the millions of people glued to the screen but all she can see is Colm's pudgy little legs swinging backwards and forwards, the grim expression on his face as she washed away the crusted blood. Replaying their conversation she realises how difficult it is, impossible almost, to think rationally about something she takes for granted. For her, being Irish is synonymous with being. Of course, when she goes home, she's aware of how anglicised her accent's getting and she's developing a sort of English reticence or so they enjoy telling her. Here it's the opposite, she's "so Irish", veiled racism or a compliment: it depends on her mood or the person saying it. And now Colm ... Maybe they should have a rule that kids of Irish and English parents have to be brought up Irish, the way the Catholic Church used insist children of mixed marriages were brought up Catholic. Olive grins at the image of her younger self, barely thirteen, jumping up in class and saying she didn't think the Catholic Church was fair. She can still see the look on the teacher's face - a nun - asking her who did she think she was questioning the Pope's teaching.

A roar from Steve startles her.

'A goal?'

Her husband sighs despondently. 'No! Bloody English are playing so they won't lose. No one's taking any chances. Look!' He glares at the screen. 'That crossball was pathetic. They should sack the manager. Y'know when England had men like Bobby Charlton, they knew what to do when they got the ball. This shower just do what they're told.'

Olive rubs her nose into his neck. She loves it when Steve gets excited over football, it reminds her of her father.

'That's Hoddle, he's good when he's playing for Tottenham. Look at him now.'

Olive half-watches, names like Danny Blanchflower, Christy Ring, shouts of 'Up Down' and 'C'mon the Dubs' echoing in her mind, the frantic pitch of Micheal O hEithir on the radio ...

'Daddy, who's winning?'

'Ssshh, go and play, there's a good girl.'

Steve slumps. 'Another example of Thatcher's Britain. Do what the Boss says even if it means annihilating yourself.'

'I'm glad. I want them to lose. C'mon Morocco!' Olive cheers but her heart isn't in it. Searching for assurance, she snuggles closer. 'Thought you wanted them to lose as well.'

'At least Morocco are trying to score,' is all Steve replies.

'If you've only joined us recently,' the commentator's voice drones, 'there's no score in this all important match but England can be admired for holding her own, down to ten men and against a Moroccan team that's used to this sort of heat.'

'Listen to that, they wouldn't say the opposite if it was raining.' Olive's about to turn away when an English player dances up the sideline, twisting and turning, outwitting the Moroccan defence.

She grabs Steve's arm. 'That's Hoddle isn't it? C'mon, Hoddle, waddle, dawdle, kick it!'

'You're getting very excited.'

'I can't bear them being such idiots- eigits,' she corrects herself.

'Cheer Morocco then.'

Olive doesn't want to admit it but she finds it hard to identify with the Moroccans. She's no stake in them, nothing to lose.

'Oh no,' Steve groans, 'they're bringing on Steven. They should put Barnes in.'

'Who's Barnes?'

'He's brilliant. Got the best goal ever scored against Brazil. Steven's a bloody midfielder.'

'What does-'

'Ssshh ... Hoddle's got it. He's going to- C'mon! C'mon! C'MON!!' Steve's voice reaches breaking point.

'Score, England, score,' Olive screams, grabbing Steve's arm, their eyes in unison following the ball as it sails through the air - and high over the net. Both sag. After a moment, Steve turns to her. 'You cheered England.'

Olive stares back at him. She feels flushed, drained, angry and ashamed all at once.

'I can't bear seeing them throwing it away. You were cheering too.'

Steve has gone back to the match, his face rigid with anticipation.

'There's only a few minutes left, they'll never ... wait, wait, Steven has it, he's going for a shot ...!'

Olive closes her eyes. 'I'm not watching. I hope they lose.' Ridiculous getting so worked up over a game. How could she explain her behaviour to Colm? Of course she knows there are thousands of Irish who follow English clubs but there are thousands who'd choke before they'd cheer an English team and she's one of them. She got carried away on Steve's excitement, that's all. Not true, a voice in her head contradicts. Admit it, you wanted England to win. Olive stiffens. C'mon, between you and me, the voice persists, sure it would be hard not to. They're your team really. You're half-English anyway, you live in England, you're married to an Englishman, Colm's-

The commentator shrieks into her reverie. Olive opens her eyes. Not trusting herself to speak, she catches Steve's eye.

'It's over. No score.'

Olive turns on her side, buries her head in a pillow. She feels sick, wishes she hadn't watched the match. Wishes she could turn back the clock. To when though? To earlier, before they'd turned on the television? To the time she collected Colm from school? Or right back to the day she married Steve, or took the boat to England? Or maybe even further: to those warm sunny days when she sat watching her daddy, asking him questions and he told her as he always did: *"Go and play, there's a good girl."*

The Spilling Of Seed

Hunching his shoulders, Owen Doherty dug his hands deep into his pockets. There had to be a way out. As his fingers played with balls of fluff in the lining, he remembered something the lads used say at school: if you do it too often hair grows on the back of your hands. At the time, the thought had scared him shitless, not enough to make him give up though. The spilling of seed: onanism. When a priest had uttered the word during a school retreat, a word Owen had never heard, shock waves had passed through him at the resemblance to his name. From bored disinterest, he'd sat bolt upright at what seemed like a message from God. A warning. So great was the impact, he'd confessed immediately and for a few weeks stopped masturbating. It didn't last. No matter how contrite he felt or how many promises he made, in the long run when the urge came he'd been unable to resist; his heart hammering until he'd found relief in a toilet, his bedroom, the coal-shed; driven sometimes to a copse of trees near his home. Once he'd done it in the living-room, his mother dozing, the excitement of being caught making his hair stand on end. In those days fear had added spice, a spice he replaced now by conjuring up ever more obscene images, images that made him feel dirty until a rush of semen washed everything away.

In the pew beside him, his mother lifted her face in devotion, the line of her mouth pinched, the hair on her upper lip quivering as she rabbited prayers. Owen closed his eyes, blotting out the black-clad figure. How could she do this to him? More to the point, why was he letting her? The answer was simple: the thought of disappointing her made him quake. As long as he could remember, it wasn't her love he'd wanted but something more allusive: her approval. To obtain it, he felt obliged to do tricks like a circus dog, go against his own nature. Ellen Doherty had made no secret of what she wanted for her son. As a youngster, he'd basked in the glow of her plans: priest, parish priest, bishop; in some of her grander schemes she had him in Rome receiving the purple. Colluding with her fantasies, never fully believing it was him she was talking about, he'd blinded himself to the fact she meant every word, that her whole life was dedicated to such an eventuality. Nothing was left to chance. From the time Owen entered secondary - private and at great sacrifice - Ellen Doherty had wheedled, cajoled, written letters, engineered meetings - all to ensure her plans reached fruition. Owen took his hands out of his pockets, stood with the rest of the congregation as Father Dundan swept out from the sacristy. Two altarboys, muddy shoes showing beneath hand-me-down soutanes, scrambled in his wake. Didn't she realise he could never be a priest, he was unfit, he'd no calling; his body, his desires cried louder than all her hopes piled together? From the altar, the priest raised a hand in blessing. Owen made the Sign of the Cross. In two weeks he'd be entering a seminary; he was eighteen, penniless and could hardly pray for a miracle.

Glory, glory, glory, Lord, God, hear my prayer, Ellen Doherty begged. Take my son, I'm offering him. Inside a hollow chest, Ellen's heart thumped. She was within a hair's breath of her heart's desire. Even so the fitness of her plans had begun to trouble her. Forgive me, she beseeched, forgive me, I've so little faith. Close as she was, Ellen worried it might not happen; feared her gift would be found unworthy. The thought wounded her. How many times in her mind's eye had she seen her son in priest's garb, received a blessing from his hands, even - God forgive her - had him anoint her with the last sacrament. If only she could look into Owen's soul, have a sign pass between them but lately she dared not glance in his direction, was afraid to catch his eye. A change had come over him. Age perhaps, but there was something else, something she caught a glimpse of now and then that made her shudder. He'd become shifty, evasive, spending long periods locked in his bedroom or out on walks, though no one ever saw him walking. It could all be traced to that filthy book: pretending he'd found it by accident; hadn't read it. Did he take her for a half-wit? For the umpteenth time she wished she'd challenged him, instead of letting embarrassment get in the way. Now she felt the stench of it whenever she went into his room. Was he pure? Glory, glory, glory, help me God, help me, to have such thoughts about someone destined to serve You, someone who'll have the power to turn bread and water into your Body and Blood. Wash away my wicked thoughts, make me pure, pure. I'm not fit to be the mother of a priest.

Surreptitiously, Owen scanned the distracted faces of the surrounding women. He knew most of them, had undressed and ravished them with his eyes. Unwittingly, they fed him, a glimpse of breast, a stain of sweat beneath an armpit, a haunch of buttocks as they bent to tie a child's shoelace, retrieve a fallen rosary. Each morsel noted, stored. Old, young, fat or thin, it didn't matter: in his day-dreams they were faceless mannequins, like the waxen dolls in McGees drapery. Owen smiled. He had Henry Miller to thank for opening his eyes. Ransacking the mobile library for a couple of books for his mother he'd happened on Tropic of Cancer. Under Travel. That was the beginning of his education and from the state of the well-thumbed pages, he was obviously not the first. He blushed suddenly, remembering the two high spots of colour on his mother's cheeks as she held the novel from her as though it were infectious. What a job he'd had convincing her it was a mistake. After that episode, he'd saved his pocket money, bought books, found safer places to hide them. He'd been so innocent at first, coming at the undoing of a button, the flick of a tongue. Nowadays his fantasies required greater imagination, more elaborate settings. New material. His eyes took up the search again and as women in the opposite aisle knelt, Owen's heart lurched as he spotted his cousin, watched her slip languidly from her seat, her plump arms coming to rest on the bench in front. Triona. Up from the country. A joke, given the size of his own village with its couple of shops and three pubs but it passed for a metropolis in these parts. Triona, he mused, was a tiny bit in love with him. Moistening dry lips, Owen dropped to the floor, his eyes latched to her body. The dress she was wearing was figured, with short, tight sleeves that bit into her flesh like the dent made by a nylon stocking. The church was cold despite the sunshine outside and the marbled skin on her bare arms and legs repelled and attracted him as he began to conjure up the rest of her body, disgusting and inviting at the same time. Slowly, he squeezed one finger, then another beneath her dress. She was a mountainy girl, bovine, milky, big-thighed.

Triona sat back. The priest was speaking but she couldn't listen, her body restless with a desire to run out of the church, gulp mouthfuls of air, dance, sing, flaunt herself to the burning sky. God, being stuck in here on a day like this, listening to the drone of an old man who'd forgotten what it was like to be young, if he'd ever known. And Owen gawking at her, with his big slimy eyes. Let him! What was it that eigit of a retreat priest had told them: when a boy looks at a girl he undresses her but when a girl looks at a boy she has romantic thoughts or yearns for a baby. Shite! She'd undressed many a man in her mind and it wasn't romance. Oh, she might be a virgin but she wasn't innocent. You'd have to be blind on a farm not to see the carry-on of animals, howling for it. Triona lowered her eyelashes. Probably wetting his pants by now. Still, he might come in handy if she could get past that witch of a mother of his with her mad notions. A priest. *Mar dhea*! God help the poor parishioners, is all anyone could say: there'd be a rake of bastards in the vicinity, that's for sure. And the way the two of them treated her. Up from the country, is it! Passing through, if only they knew. Still, he wasn't bad looking though he'd probably come in a flash. She knew all about his type from magazines.

Ellen's eyes did the rounds, stopping at the sight of exposed flesh. There she was, the fat lump, showing herself off for the whole world to gape at. Had that niece of hers no respect for the House of God? She must remember to have a chat with Triona after mass, explain the decencies; someone had to keep an eye on the hussy. Her poor mother, a holy woman and sick all her life, would thank her for it. Maybe it was a mistake not letting her lodge with them, that Mags creature she was staying with was a bit too easy-going. Still, she couldn't run the risk: a girl of seventeen, even a cousin, in the same house as a boy off to be a priest! Perish the thought. She'd seen her all the same, batting her eyes. No shame. Acting the innocent but it didn't fool her. Her son would be a fine catch - Dear God, she should be praying, not thinking like this. Where was her charity? Hail Mary bless and look after all young people especially- A thought dried the words in her throat. What if the pair were in love? The 'come-on' looks hadn't been all one way, she'd seen that too. Her heart shrank. Love was the cause of every misfortune. That was something she could vouch for from bitter experience. Unsettled, Ellen opened her missal but instead of an image of Christ, the bloated face of her husband smirked out at her. Bartley. Dead and gone where he could do no harm. Or was he? Had she not begun to spot traces of him in Owen's demeanour? The boy's mother snapped shut the prayer book, drew her lips tight. Promises had to be kept. During her hour of need, she'd prayed for deliverance, pledged her son, all she had to offer. God had answered in His own mysterious way, taking Bartley in his prime. He had fulfilled His side of the bargain - now it was her turn.

America danced in front of Owen's eyes. America was where he wanted to go. A country that had elected an Irishman president - that was the place to be. Yes, the States was the land of opportunity, you could become somebody there, no matter who you started out as. Wasn't Kennedy living proof of that? Last year, the whole village had crowded into McDaid's to see Kennedy step from a plane on his first trip to Ireland. His mother might turn him into a priest, she'd enough determination, but whatever happened he'd no intention of staying in a dump like this! He hated the place, every last cow shed and dunghill. Stuck in a time warp. Crawling with people who couldn't say hello without going back to your seed and breed. Who was his seed? A good-for-nothing drunk, dead by the time Owen had reached his fourth birthday. He'd hardly known him, but he'd heard stories: drinking bouts, the fierce temper, fists, women. Through interlocked fingers, Owen watched his mother close her prayer book. He found it impossible to reconcile this demon of a man with the woman kneeling beside him. Had they been in love? Courted? His name was never mentioned in the house, there were no photographs. Owen sank into his hands. She had done her best to erase his father from their lives but Bartley's genes were in Owen's body and there was nothing she could do about that.

Father Dundan turned his back on the congregation. Sighed. He'd been saying Mass at this same altar for thirty years, would probably go on saying it until he died. Not that he believed in what he was doing. All habit. But habits die hard. Perhaps he should ask for a transfer. Go someplace, somewhere he'd have time to think, to make peace with God. He still believed in Him - that wasn't the problem. It was himself he didn't believe in. And his parishioners knew it. They still came in their droves, would for another ween of years, but their children's children? The young were drifting, lads staying in bed with hangovers, girls coming to church half-dressed. No respect. When you lose the women you lose the whole shebang. They're the mainstay. Women like Ellen Doherty. Her life blood sapped by the Church. Mass everyday and hoping to turn that sly son of hers into a priest. As if prayer alone could do it. Still, he mustn't complain, she did the altar, arranged the flowers, would be here like clockwork this afternoon to help with Benediction. Making a mental note to ask her about candles, he bent, kissed the chalice then turned and faced his people. His eyes settled on the black-clad woman. No compassion, he thought. No love. Driven out of her by a shambles of a marriage. Not like ... his gaze shifted to Triona. Is it a second-cousin or niece? Now there's life. There's a girl could warm the cockles of a man's heart. 'Benediction,' he announced, 'will be at five o'clock. Among those we are asked to pray for this week are Joseph McLoughlin ...'

Triona thought about the envelope stuffed under her mattress. Enough to get to England and from there who knows - America maybe. She couldn't go alone. Her brothers would track her down, drag her home in disgrace. She needed someone to go with her. That eigit of a cousin wanted out but had he the nerve? She'd nerve enough for the two of them if he were willing. Was he still watching her? Glancing over, she met his fierce stare. Their eyes locked then Triona dropped her gaze as her Aunt Ellen's head turned in her direction. He's mine, she thought, if I play my cards right. And I can dump him later if it doesn't work out.

Above the shuffling and coughing, Father Dundan raised a hand in blessing, dismissing the churchgoers with a nod of satisfaction. Leaving the altar, he motioned one of the servers. 'Run and catch Ellen Doherty, tell her I need to speak to her. Be quick. I want my breakfast.'

Triona lingered by the chapel gates; seeing Owen hurry towards her, his hand waving her to wait, she began walking slowly ahead, a smile dimpling her cheeks. He was ripe for the picking all right. There was a bus leaving for Dublin at five this afternoon although it would be a great pity to miss Benediction. There was nothing she adored more than the smell of incense.

Betrayal

'Your breakfast's getting cold,' Rita complains, clicking her tongue before she can stop herself. Fingers holding the newspaper tighten. Behind it her husband's eyes gleam.

'More tea?' she inquires in a placating tone.

Fergal nods, folding the paper, propping it against a vase of artificial flowers. Rita pours, watching the arc of liquid darken as she raises the pot to prevent the leaves clogging. Her husband manoeuvres a fork-full of bacon and egg into his mouth, washes it down with tea, which he takes black, his attention absorbed by the article he's reading. Rita pulls her dressing-gown tighter, wraps a hand round her cup for warmth. Part of a headline is visible: GOVERNMENT TRI- -bunal, she completes in her head. Another one! Fat lot of good they do, except make lawyers richer. A thousand euros a day some of them earn. More. What do they do with all that money? Tightness grips her chest. Strange. In the past things like that never bothered her. A smaller headline distracts her: RACE ATTACK. Rita tuts; shakes her head. There's always people worse off, she consoles herself. She feels sorry for immigrants, the women especially, with their big soulful eyes, prams laden with kids, like throwbacks to an another era. She squints at the small print. Two young men being questioned. The youths hurled- Rita averts her gaze, shudders. Disgusting. Thank God both her boys are safely married. She stirs the dregs of her tea, aware of Fergal rising from the table. In a moment, he'll cross to the mirror, adjust his tie, re-adjust it, then pick up his briefcase, tap it for no reason. His movements have become predictable, Rita knows them inside out. As he examines his reflection, she slips up behind him without a sound, the two ends of his tie suddenly in her hands as she pulls, tight, tighter ... The kitchen door shuts with a slam. Rita unclenches her fists. What's got into her lately? She must be watching too much telly. Sighing, she begins clearing the breakfast things, looking to see if he's taken the newspaper. In the old days, he'd leave it for her occasionally. A gesture. Recently, he's given up all pretence. Is barely civil. Blames her really. Agitated, she levers a rind of bacon from his plate, scrapes at the bits of congealed egg. No point in putting them in dirty. She'll only have to do them again. The journey to the kitchen takes her past a wall of framed photographs: communions, confirmations, graduations, weddings. A lifetime frozen. She tries not to think about the missing photo, its imprint still visible on the wallpaper.

"Her name is not to be mentioned in this house. Is that understood?"

Rita hasn't heard from her daughter in years, not since Fergal threw her out. Where is Jennifer? And the baby? A teenager by now. As tears threaten, her eyes swivel to the face of her younger self, a woman brimming with love, confetti dotting the veil covering her hair, each sequin a dream hoping to be realised. How can things change so utterly? The question is part of the daily babble in her head, a babble that goes round and round without ... She hurries to the kitchen, hands trembling as she loads the dishwasher. Get a move on, she reprimands herself, or you'll be late for mass.

In the street, leaves swirl and dance round the ankles of passers-by or flatten themselves against coats in a futile effort to keep airborne. Rita flips one away, keeps walking. A little way along, a boy leans against a wall, legs sprawled, fag dangling. His eyes flick here, there, nowhere. She gives him a wide berth, her hand tightening on the strap of her imitation leather bag. Let him try. All he'd get would be rosary beads, cheap ones at that, her good pair with the mother of pearl cross are at home, safe under her pillow. Her purse is safe too, nestling in the side pocket of her coat. She pats it with her free hand, allows herself a satisfied smile. Even so, the need for deception annoys her. There was a time if you dropped money in this street, someone would pick it up, return it to you. When she was growing up, just a few blocks away, this road with its spacious red-bricked houses was considered desirable. As a young woman, she'd dreamed of living in one of them; convinced the poshness would rub off; would have the power to change her. The day her and Fergal had put a down payment, she'd danced for joy. But the magic hadn't worked. Within a few years, those affluent enough had sold up, moved to better parts of the city. The houses were turned into flats, nobody knew who their neighbour was. A young fella up for a football match had been kicked to death just round the corner. Local men were involved. A sour taste rises in Rita's mouth, her heartbeat quickens. Little by little, everything she loves, even the streets, are being taken from her. Buffeted by wind, she grips at some railings for support. Ahead, the solid grey mass of St Stephen's is visible.

The priest holds up the chalice. A bell rings. Body and Blood. Rita strikes her breast but the sense of peace she'd been hoping for eludes her. Over joined hands, she studies the bowed heads of the handful of women dotting the church, wonders what's going on behind the placid faces, the supplicant eyes.

'Excuse me.'

Rita flattens herself to let a woman pass, follows her out to join the small queue waiting to receive. Back at her seat, she recites prayers learned in childhood but a feeling of emptiness engulfs her, the words she is saying so much wasted breath. She sits up. The first time this had happened she'd mentioned it to a priest in confession; his advice had been to go on praying, to pray and pray, no matter what she was feeling. Her soul, he'd assured her, would reap the benefit just as seeds take in nourishment during the long, lean months of winter. Remembering his words, she prays, tries to grasp the miracle she's just partaken in. The Body and Blood of Christ. Does she believe? She's not sure. The miracle she longs for is much more ordinary: to see her daughter again, her grandchild; to be able to communicate with her husband. Rita seeks out the body of Christ hanging above the altar, contemplates the wounds, the blood trickling from His head, the nails in His hands and feet. She recalls that when a soldier thrust a sword into His side, water poured forth: His Blood had been shed, He had no more to give. Dutifully, she rises as the priest leaves the altar.

'Morning, Mrs Dunne, blustery old weather?'

Rita stares at the blood on the butcher's apron.

'I hope Father Byrne gave you something to think about this morning?'

'Oh, he doesn't bother with us oulwans. Saves it for Sundays. Any chops, Bob?'

'Lovely ones, just in. I'll say this Mrs Dunne, that husband of yours eats like a king. Two, is it?'

'And some kidneys - he fancies them of a morning sometimes.'

'Like a king,' the butcher repeats, running his eyes along the trays, selecting two large chops, lean ones with the fat trimmed.

Through a half-open door, carcasses of meat are visible, naked, obscene-looking. Seeing them Rita's reminded of the crucifix above the altar. Does Bob cut them up himself? How do ordinary people do things like that? She has a dim memory of calves giddying across a field, a holiday in the country when she was young. She tries to remember where, can't. Voices slide into her thoughts. Rita glances over her shoulder, sees a black woman standing in the doorway. The woman is talking loudly to a lighter-skinned man, gesticulating, as if trying to explain something. Rita turns away, afraid the woman might think she's staring, then turns back, half-smiles, not wanting her to think she minds.

'That'll be six seventy.' Bob tells her, wrapping the meat. He gestures towards the black couple. 'Everything's changing, isn't it Mrs Dunne? Our own's not our own anymore.'

Rita puzzles his words. Perhaps he objects to them being here, imagines she does. She hesitates. Bob's a fixture in her life, he looks out for her, gives her bargains, she wouldn't like to offend him. All the same they're God's creatures. Wasn't Jesus dark skinned? He'd have to be, coming from that part of the world. Confused, she fiddles with her purse, tries to think of a way to convey her muddled thoughts.

'The old lock rusty, Mrs Dunne? Course you can't be too careful these days. Never know who's about.' He grins coldly at the waiting couple. 'Get you something? Speaka English?'

Angry with Bob for involving her, Rita hands him seven euro. In her hurry to be gone, she grabs at the meat, feels the package slip from her hands. As it hits the tiled floor the bag splits, revealing its bright red contents. Rita feels faint. Holding her hand to her forehead, she bends, finds herself eyeball to eyeball with the black woman.

'Don't touch it!' Rita screams. The woman springs back.

Bob comes from behind the counter. 'Want me to change them?'

'There's no need,' she assures him.

'At least let me wrap them up again.'

While he fiddles with a new bag, Rita tries to engineer an opportunity to smile at the black woman, to apologise. But the woman refuses to meet her gaze, turns her head away disdainfully.

'Don't go off without your change,' Bob calls, handing her a few coins.

Shoving them in her bag, Rita stumbles out into the day.

'A funny thing happened-'

'-Tea,' Fergal interrupts, looking up from the paper. Rita pours. Steam from the pot fogs his glasses. Exasperated, he takes them off, cleans them. Rita feels a coldness in her chest, like an iceberg pushing its way to her throat. She takes a deep breath. The iceberg melts and a trickle of something she recognises as hatred courses through her. On the breadboard, the knife glints. Rita runs from the room to the hallway. She can't breathe, her heart is jumping from her body. I'm having a heart attack, she thinks. Jesus, Mary and Joseph, help me. She grabs her bag from the end of the banister, pulls out her rosary. There's a clink as change from the butcher's falls to the floor. Light-headed, Rita gazes down at the three ten cent pieces at her feet.

Rita returns to the kitchen. The loaf's sitting where she left it, the bread-knife alongside. In what seems like slow motion, she picks it up, sees blood splatter on the white tablecloth. It soaks in, spreads, grows fainter. She remembers a bouquet of red roses someone gave her once, the petals fading, falling.

'Mother of God,' Fergal screams, 'have you gone mad altogether!'

Rita stares at her wrist, wonders how long before water appears.

Butterflies

The gobs of jelly were alive, teeming with maggoty things, squirming, wriggling, their shiny pinheads rearing out of the slime. Lisa gawked, open-mouthed. On the tallest nettles, larger grubs, inky, ribbed, each with a shimmer of opaque spots, sidled along ragged, hairy leaves. Lisa adopted one, cheering it on as it shunted its small pulsing body. Reaching the edge, the maggot wavered, grappling like a punch-drunk boxer for something to cling to, a path to the next leaf, to food, safety, life. Butterflies, Lisa marvelled, who'd believe such ugly yokes could turn into butterflies? The thought blazed, warming her, before an urge to cry quenched it. She kicked at the nettles, trampling on the nearest ones until she remembered Mrs Lacey would be waiting. With a last half-hearted kick, she began to run as if someone was catching up on her, was about to pounce, the drumming of her heels echoing the beat of her heart, blotting out thought.

Lisa stuffed two biscuits into her mouth, poured the coke into a glass. Her gaze lingered over the sparkling hob, the brightly-coloured tiles behind the sink unit, the shelf of cookery books, each with a shiny cover. Perfect. The kind of kitchen she'd have when she grew up. Of course, she'd have to marry someone like Mr Lacey. An agony of hope gripped the girl's heart at the thought the vet might walk though the door any second. Lisa was in love with Mr Lacey (Aidan, she called him in her day-dreams), had been since the moment he'd smiled at her, the moment she'd realised he was in love with her. Not that he'd said anything but then she was only twelve. There were plenty of hints though. Lisa stroked the contours of the little plastic sheep he'd given her. The ornament was her prize possession, she carried it everywhere, slept with it under her pillow. And wasn't he always admiring her hair or asking what she was going to be when she grew up? Lisa hoped he understood why she stammered, blushed, but of course he had to pretend not to notice, otherwise Mrs Lacey might get jealous. Lisa loved Mrs Lacey. More, maybe. It was a different kind of love, not one that set her heart thumping although it filled her with longing all the same. Hearing a gurgle in the hall, the rosiness in Lisa's world faded. Why had Patrick the luck to be born a Lacey? In a flash, Lisa grasped it was all chance: chance who you were born, chance if you survived. Like the butterfly grubs. It wasn't fair, she thought, not fair at all.

'Eat up all those biscuits,' Mrs Lacey ordered in her jokey-earnest voice, bustling into the kitchen. 'Look, who's here,' she addressed the ten month-old baby nestling in her arms. Seeing the girl, the child turned away, burrowed into his mother's breast.

'I don't know what's got into Patrick, making strange. Sure you know Lisa,' she tickled him.

'He'll be all right once you've gone.' Lisa assured her.

'Must be a phase he's going through,' the child's mother shrugged. 'Mummy has to go into town. Be a good boy now,' she chided playfully.

The girl nibbled a Mikado, leaving the jammy bit until last. Coming up for air, Patrick spied the biscuits, reached out a chubby hand.

'Not for you, Patikins,' the woman cooed. 'I'll put him in his buggy, you can take him for a walk later.'

Finishing her drink, Lisa wiped a slick of wet from her lips.

'You know where the stuff is if he needs changing.'

Having settled the baby, Mrs Lacey crossed to a mirror. For a few moments, she studied her face, pinching her cheeks, fluffing her hair, puckering her lips as if about to kiss someone. Grimacing, she fished a lipstick from her bag, began applying colour, stretching her mouth, pursing and smacking. Lisa followed each movement, mentally practising, learning to be a woman, just as she'd been doing since the day she was born.

Lisa shut the bedroom door. Her mammy was right, she was wicked; she deserved to be punished, deserved to go to Hell. And just because girls in her class said it was all made up didn't mean it didn't exist. She'd read about Hell: a place where you burned forever, your skin shrivelled, black. Lisa dug a fingernail into her wrist, ignoring the pain until a crescent of blood appeared. Today was definitely the last time. Imagine what would happen if she was found out? The thought filled her with dread. She wouldn't do it again, ever. To show she wasn't pretending, Lisa decided to make a pact, give up something really important. What, she wondered, chewing the end of a biro. Aidan, she'd give up Aiden. From now on, she wouldn't let herself think about him, wouldn't imagine his arms reaching for her, his lips brushing hers. She tore a page from one of her jotters: writing things out gave them more power. As she scribbled, the sound of running water filled the room.

'Lisa, Lisa, come here,' her mother's voice echoed through the silent house.

The girl put her hands to her ears.

'Lis-saa,' the voice shrilled, 'I'm running your bath.'

Making a ball of the paper, Lisa flung it on the floor. Stupid bitch, thinking words could change anything. This was her life. Chance or not - what difference did it make?

Mrs Whelan stepped aside to let her daughter pass.

'I had a bath yesterday,' the girl protested.

'Watch your tongue. At this time of year you need one everyday,'

Lisa undressed, aware of her mother's rigid face, her accusing eyes.

'Look at you, skinny as a rake, you'll never have half the figure I had.'

Stepping out of her clothes, she slipped into the water. The woman lit a cigarette, sat on the toilet seat, puffing. 'If I didn't look after you, you'd be stinking to high heaven. You know that, don't you?'

Lisa nodded.

'I asked a question.'

'Yes, Mammy.'

Smoke and steam clouded the tiled room making it dreamy. Dreamy and horrible. Her mother pulled on the cigarette until the tip glowed, flakes of ash floating in the moist air, clinging to the woman's hair, dress, falling to the floor.

'Hurry up, d'you want the water to get cold?'

Lisa began to scrub, tearing at her skin with a cloth. With a satisfied grunt, her mother turned on a tap, held the cigarette under. Hearing a faint sizzle, Lisa exhaled.

'How can you wash your private parts like that? Stand up.'

The girl obeyed, spreading her hands, covering herself as best she could.

'You know what happens to girls who don't wash. Maggots grow. Is that what you want?'

'Leave me alone,' Lisa begged, 'I'll wash properly, I promise.' The word turned to a shriek as a hand struck her buttocks.

'Cheek, that's all I get for caring about you!' The hand struck again. 'It's for your own good Lisa.'

'I'm sorry, Mammy,' Lisa wailed. 'I'm sorry.'

The woman slumped, drifted off. When she turned to face her daughter again, she looked young, soft. 'Who loves you?' she asked.

'You do, Mammy,' Lisa sobbed.

'There, there, Mammy loves you,' her mother crooned, wrapping a towel tightly round the wet girl. Swaddled, Lisa felt the hardness of the woman's body, hard and unyielding but all she had to cling to.

On her way to Lacey's next morning, Lisa stopped in the waste ground. Millions of caterpillars were crawling over the nettles, nibbling, gorging, making lacework of the weeds. At some point, they would turn into chrysalises, then butterflies. When that happened, if one flew into her garden, there would be no way of knowing if it was one of the insects she was looking at now: ugly, earthbound, revolting.

Lisa undressed Patrick. She hadn't made the pact and now she'd got this far, there was no going back. Why should Patrick escape? It probably didn't hurt anyway. Babies cried for no reason, her mother said. And Aidan didn't love her. Earlier, he'd barely noticed her in the kitchen, shouted when she'd asked a question. After he'd gone out, Mrs Lacey had been all apologies, explaining how he'd been up all night with a sick horse and to make matter worse Patrick wasn't sleeping, was keeping them both awake. Lisa sneered. What did she care if they never slept? Serve them right. Them and their stupid baby. Always making a fuss of it. Ugly, fat lump. Pleased to be out of his nappy, Patrick kicked blindly. Sprawled on the mat, arms and legs stretched, he reminded Lisa of a photograph she'd seen of a butterfly pinned to a board. 'Who's a bold boy?' she asked, reaching for the little floppy worm, caressing it gently. As the baby stiffened, Lisa pulled until he screamed. Turning him over, she slapped his bottom, once, twice. He howled, snotty tears rolling down his cheeks. 'No crying!' she ordered, raising a hand. 'I'm warning you.' Patrick sucked in his breath, whimpered, plump arms treading air. A wave of power surged through Lisa. Lifting the boy, she held him to her, soothing him with all the words she could think of. He was hers, hers, she loved him. Only she could make him feel better.

Lisa lay curled up in bed, the curtains closed, a ribbon of light where they didn't meet. The caterpillars had vanished. She'd gone to check and there was nothing left but wisps of black stuff. She'd vanish too as soon as she was old enough, her old clothes the only proof she'd ever existed. She'd never see her mammy or the Lacey's again. Somewhere, far, far away, where nobody knew her, she'd find a place to live, turn into someone else. Through the open window came the sound of small animals scurrying. Birds flying home. Calling. The room darkened. Grew still. In the stillness, something gossamer unfolded, made for the gap in the curtains. Caught in a ray of light, it fluttered. Lisa pulled the duvet over her head, waited for the tears to stop.